Like Casablanca

SYLVIA MASSARA

License Notes

This novel is entirely a work of fiction. The names, characters, and incidents portrayed in it are the work of the author's imagination. Any resemblance to actual persons, living or dead, events, or localities is entirely coincidental.

Published by Tudor Enterprises
Australia
(61) 419 492 623

Revised edition 2016
First published by
Tudor Enterprises in 2013

ISBN-13: 978-0-9808350-5-2

DEDICATION

For Dad, Henry, and Lofty,
You are missed, but are always present in my heart.

Titles by Sylvia Massara

Romantic comedy:

Like Casablanca
The Other Boyfriend

General fiction:

The Soul Bearers

Mia Ferrari mystery series:

Playing With The Bad Boys
The Gay Mardi Gras Murders
The South Pacific Murders

Sci-fi romance:

The Stranger

For more information on Massara's novels, both in eBook
& paperback editions, plus participating retailers;
or for latest novels or to contact the author, please visit:

www.sylviamassara.com

CHAPTER 1

I wrote my first blog today. I thought it sucked, but Scotty loved it. He looked up from the laptop screen, turned to me with his wide, knee-jerking smile, and winked.

"Darling, you've got a winner," he declared in a sexy baritone voice.

I gazed at him in wonder, momentarily lost in the blue of his gorgeous eyes. Too bad he was gay.

"Do you really think so?" I wasn't sure if I should take his compliment at face value. He was, after all, my best friend and bound to be biased. I didn't have time to muse about this for long, however, because I was distracted by the tinkling of the bell above the shop door, announcing we had a customer. Scotty rushed forward to greet them, and I was left alone with my thoughts even though my eyes followed him.

The customer was a well-dressed, elderly woman who seemed to fall under Scotty's spell immediately. He had that effect on people, both gay and straight. I smiled—if only I could say the same thing for myself.

After my recent break up with Josh, I wasn't sure I "had it" anymore; but I didn't even want to go there right now—better to stay focused on my blog. While Scotty helped his customer with a Queen Anne cake platter, I leaned on the shop counter where the laptop rested and read from the screen.

1

Cat Ryan's Dating Blog #1

Gen Yers are doing it! So why not us old fogies? Yes, you guessed it. I'm talking about internet dating. Now, before you recoil in horror, keep an open mind and read on. The worst that can happen is you will learn something new.

What's so special about internet dating? Well, for one thing, it is low cost as opposed to going through a professional dating agency that will often charge exorbitant fees and put you through a bunch of psychological profiling questionnaires—only to end up matching you with your ex-husband. And before you snicker and shake your head in disbelief, let me assure you this is true. Why do I know this? Because it happened to me—and what are the chances? A million to one, right? And yet, it happened, and I didn't even get my $3000 fee refunded. So my advice is: STAY AWAY FROM DATING AGENCIES!

Another reason why internet dating is so cool is that you have a chance to shop around and get a feel for the person before you meet them. You can check out their profile, see their photo, and even chat with them online. So you might say you get to test drive the car before you buy it.

Not too bad. It didn't suck after all, although I wasn't exactly over the moon with it; but it wasn't at all bad. Plus the bit about being matched with the ex was true.

When I was in my late twenties, and my marriage of two years broke up, I went to a dating agency at the urging of my friends. Just as I wrote in my blog, after a series of tests with a relationships counsellor—because the agency claimed they wanted to get a feel for their clients—I was matched with my commitment-phobic ex-husband. After this, I gave up on the whole thing.

The agency had promised six introductions to professional men for a total fee of $3000. This was an exclusive agency, not one that introduced you to riffraff; but hey, they introduced me to my ex, and while he was a professional businessperson, he was still riffraff as far as I was concerned.

The old lady let out a whoop of delight, startling me, and I looked up to see her hand resting on Scotty's forearm. "You're so naughty! Look at me, I'm blushing," she exclaimed.

I assumed he had paid her some outrageous compliment. Scotty

2

was like that. It was all part of his charm. He patted the lady's hand and then picked up a lovely Art Deco mirror in the shape of a half moon. The lady's eyes lit up at the sight of it, and I knew Scotty had made another sale. Smiling, I looked back down at the computer screen.

The rest of my blog went on to discuss statistics I had researched about the increasing number of Gen Xers and Baby Boomers who were following this new trend and giving online dating a go. Then, I finished off with some dos and don'ts to keep in mind when dating through the net.

Scotty came back to ring the sales through the cash register, and I slipped out to the small office at the back of the shop to make us some coffee. When the customer left, I handed him a cup before remarking, "So how many items did you sell to that poor woman?"

His dazzling smile almost knocked me over with the power of its sex appeal, and I had to remind myself, yet again, that he was gay.

Scotty and I had known each other for years. We met at an antiques fair, and he had asked me to work part-time at his shop. It was a match made in heaven—it gave him the chance to go to auctions and estate sales; and me, what I called a "bread and butter" job while I wrote my book on Renaissance art.

From day one, Scotty and I became fast friends, and of late, he had come in very handy when I needed a date after the break up with my ex-fiancé, Josh. My heart contracted with pain for a moment at the thought of him, but I quickly refocused my attention back to Scotty.

"She purchased the cake platter, the mirror, and an exquisite Clarice Cliff tea set," he replied, pleased with himself. "Oh, and speaking of tea sets..." He disappeared for a few moments, only to return with a lovely far-eastern tea set, complete with a small brass platter, which served as a tabletop set on a hand-worked wooden stand. "What do you think?" He set down the small table in front of me.

I took in the wonderful craftsmanship of the pieces. The engraved brass tray had intricate motifs complementing the hand-carved, wooden base with its musharabi decorations. A silver teapot with hand-worked legs and a high conical lid completed the set along with six glasses, worked in colours of red, green, and blue on the top half of each delicately carved glass. It was a beautiful set.

"Moroccan caravan tea set?" I ventured.

Scotty nodded, rapture in his eyes. "Darling, it's at least two hundred years old."

"Wow! I love it. Where did you find it?" I ran my fingers gently along the intricately carved wooden stand.

"Estate sale in Forestville. Remember the one I went to about a month ago?"

I nodded while I picked up one of the tea glasses. The piece was fragile, the glass wafer-thin. "Well, I have to say, it's absolutely gorgeous."

"I know. Rick's going to love it."

"One of your private clients, I take it?" I queried. Scotty always scouted around for unique acquisitions for his regular clientele. He had a long list of wealthy buyers and collectors.

"Yes," Scotty replied, the look on his face one of romantic contemplation.

I laughed. "You're a big flirt, Scotty. What about the delectable Mark, where is he these days?" Mark was Scotty's on-again, off-again boyfriend.

"You're jumping to conclusions too fast, as always," Scotty remarked derisively.

I rolled my eyes and sighed. "So you keep telling me, but what am I supposed to think when you look like you've seen a young version of George Michael?"

He turned his nose up at me. "Okay, I'm putting this back now." He picked up the tea set and walked away.

I knew he was just pretending to be upset, so I followed him as he headed toward a corner of the shop where he stored pieces already spoken for behind a large, hand-painted, Chinese screen.

"So what's going on?" I uttered, curiosity getting the better of me.

"Well, if you must know, Rick is the owner of Rick's Café," he stated as if I was supposed to know the significance of this. Scotty sighed at my look of ignorance. "Like Casablanca," he added and waited for me to react.

I still didn't know what he was trying to say. "Okay. So?"

He threw his hands up in the air and made his way back to the sales counter with me in tow. "Honestly, darling, where have you been?"

4

"Too busy wallowing in self-pity," I answered before I could help myself.

Scotty saw the threat of tears in my eyes and dropped his guise of indignation. "Oh, come here. Come to Scotty." His arms beckoned me.

I sniffed back the tears and moved into the circle of his arms for one of his comforting hugs. It was wonderful to be held by a gorgeous man—even one who was my dear friend, and aside from our friendship was not in the least bit interested in me. Still, it was good for the sake of my self-esteem. Josh had really done a job on me.

"I know it's only been a few months," Scotty comforted me, "but you're just going to have to make an effort to move on. I mean, look at you, you're an attractive woman who can have any man."

Not quite, I thought. I couldn't have Josh, so what was the point of being attractive? Josh had said I was beautiful. Yet, this hadn't stopped him from cheating on me.

"Perhaps you'll meet someone through this internet dating project of yours," Scotty commented.

My head shot up and I stepped away from his embrace. "Now, let's get one thing straight. I only picked up this gig because my ex-editor wanted me to do a bit of freelancing for the magazine's blog."

Prior to my decision to write a book, I had been writing for a women's magazine as a regular contributor. The magazine ran a popular blog and they were now doing a series of articles on internet dating. My editor, with whom I still kept in touch, had contacted me to see if I was interested in doing the blog posts. The money was good, and every little bit helped.

After my break up with Josh, I'd had to move out of his lovely Double Bay townhouse, and all I could afford to rent was a small studio atop an art gallery near Scotty's shop in Paddington. At the time, Scotty suggested I move in with him and share his beautiful terrace house, but I didn't want to get in the way of him and his stormy relationship with Mark, so I opted for living nearby instead.

Though Mark was a flight attendant and hardly ever around, I would've felt like a third wheel had I moved in. The fact that I would've been around them all the time might have had an effect on my friendship with Scotty and this, I didn't want to risk.

The blog gig was for a period of three months, and I had to

5

write one blog post per week plus reply to any comments from readers. The editor wanted me to date men I met through the internet and write about my experiences. In exchange for this, I was paid five hundred dollars per blog post. Not bad; even if it was going to be a short-lived job. If the blog started to get plenty of hits, though, the editor gave me to understand that she might extend the timeframe. This was welcome news seeing as I was now paying for rent, groceries, and bills whereas when I had lived with Josh, I had paid nothing.

Josh hadn't wanted me to pay for anything, perhaps out of guilt, so up to then my part-time job at Scotty's shop had been more than enough to provide me with personal expense money while I worked on my book. Then, things changed. I had only been living with Josh for about a year when I became aware of his infidelity and left him.

Fortunately, Scotty was able to give me a few more hours of work per week, which helped with my finances. The blogging work really came in as a bonus. So I had managed to cope financially since my break up—only just.

"I know you're not really ready to date yet," Scotty stated, unaware of my thoughts. "All I'm saying is you should keep an open mind. You just never know whom you're going to meet out there." He grabbed hold of my arm and marched me to stand in front of a gilt-edged Venetian mirror. "Look at yourself. You're young and vibrant. What man wouldn't want to go out with you?"

I attempted a smile as I took in my appearance: almond-shaped green eyes looked back from a youngish face, framed by short blonde hair. High cheekbones and a pair of pouty lips completed the picture. "I have crow's feet," I announced petulantly.

Scotty laughed. "You're joking, right?"

I shook my head. No, I wasn't joking. I was ageing!

"You're crazy, darling," Scotty exclaimed. "You're blessed with the best features of both your parents—Italian complexion from your mother, silky soft and olive skinned, and gorgeous green eyes from your Irish father."

I added in a caustic tone, "And beautiful blonde hair from the hairdresser in order to hide the emerging grey." I tried to smile, but my lips had other ideas, and I looked like a sad smiley icon.

"Okay, so what?" Scotty remarked. "We all need a bit of cosmetic help from time to time." He only said this because he had

6

just turned thirty and was in his prime, while I was on the cusp of forty. I moved away from the mirror and went back to the sales counter.

"You didn't finish telling me about the Casablanca thing," I reminded him, trying to steer his attention away from the topic of dating and my looks.

"That's right." He glanced at his cup. "How about a refill first while I finish off with my paperwork? Then, I'll tell you all about it."

As it turned out, he didn't get a chance to tell me anything because another customer walked in, and the rest of the day kept us busy. By the time we had a chance to stop and take a breather it was close to five in the afternoon.

"I'm going to an interstate auction on Thursday," Scotty announced. "Then, I'll be taking the weekend off and staying on in Brisbane. Mark's flying in, and we need some time together. I was wondering if you'd housesit for me and look after Henry."

"Sure," I replied without hesitation. After all, I had nothing planned, except to work on my next blog post and try to set up an internet date so I would have something to write about. "Do you want me to keep the shop open right through?" The weekend was the busiest time for us.

"If you don't mind," he answered. "I'll pay you overtime."

"No need," I replied. "Just pay me the normal rate. Remember, I'll be living at your place and making sure I eat you out of house and home," I put in mischievously.

Scotty was a fair boss, and he had been so wonderful to me since the break up that I didn't have the heart to accept extra payment for working on a weekend. Besides, between customers, I would be writing my blog post.

"By the way, has anything changed in Henry's diet?" Henry was Scotty's big marmalade cat, who was spoiled rotten, but lovable all the same. Scotty loved the cat as if it was his own child, and being an animal lover myself, I could relate. Besides, I was Henry's honorary aunt, as Scotty put it. Henry was soft and fluffy, and a hell of a lot better company than Josh had ever been.

"Diet's the same; kangaroo meat one day and tuna the next; kibble all day long with plenty of drinking water."

It was cold out, even though we were in the middle of spring, so I put on my coat and picked up my handbag in preparation to leave.

"Okay. Have a good trip and give my regards to Mark."

Scotty looked up from his paperwork. "Will do. But before you go, can you do me a favour on Friday after you close the shop?"

I nodded.

"I need you to deliver the tea set to Rick." Scotty wrote out the contact details and address of the customer. "I told him I'd do it, but now I'm not going to be here."

"Fine, I'll do it." I took the paper from him and reading the client's name, Rick Blake, I added with sudden understanding, "Ah, no wonder he named his place Rick's Café. It's his name. Just change a few letters at the end of the surname and you get *Rick Blaine* from *Casablanca*." I was referring to the name of the character played by Humphrey Bogart in the movie.

"That's what I was trying to tell you," Scotty stated. "And Rick's not gay, by the way." He gave me a knowing look that made me sigh with impatience. He never gave up.

"Forget it," I chided him. "If you're trying to—"

"I'm not trying anything," he interrupted. "It's just a big coincidence about the movie and all that. Plus Rick's from New York, just like *Rick Blaine*.

"Big deal," I returned, dismissing the whole thing. "Lots of people are from New York."

Scotty threw me a dazzling smile, which only served to remind me how sex-starved I was. "Sure lots of people are from New York, but not many are named Rick Blake and have a café called Rick's. I'm telling you, it's just like Casablanca."

I rolled my eyes and grabbed the spare set of keys from the register drawer. "Have a nice trip." I planted a kiss on his cheek on my way out.

Outside, as I clutched the lapels of my coat close to my breast in order to keep out the chill wind, an image of Bogie popped into my head, and I started to walk down the street humming "As Time Goes By".

CHAPTER 2

Henry eyed me with a calculating look in his amber glare; then he jumped up on the suede camel-coloured lounge. He proceeded to turn repeatedly in circles while he tested the softness of the sofa with his paws before nestling down against my thigh. He would have settled on my lap if I hadn't had my laptop resting on it.

"Does your father let you climb on the furniture?" I asked the fluffy orange cat as he groomed himself, starting with his front paws. "Stupid question, of course. You probably own this whole place, right?"

Looking up at me for the briefest of moments, the cat returned to his grooming as if to say, "Ask a stupid question, and you'll get a stupid answer."

I turned my attention back to the computer screen to read through yet another profile on the internet dating site. I had been at this since I finished dinner two hours earlier and out of the tens of profiles I read through, I couldn't settle on anyone in particular. My second blog post was due in the next few days, and I still didn't have a date. I sighed with exasperation and looked around the room in order to distract myself from my gloomy thoughts.

Being an antiques lover, one would think Scotty possessed an antique-style home. Surprisingly, his terrace in Paddington had been renovated to reflect modern, contemporary décor with off-white walls and a white ceiling sprinkled with down lights, shining on cinnamon-coloured New Zealand wool carpet. The house consisted of a large rectangular lounge room, a medium-sized formal dining room, an eat-in kitchen downstairs, and three bedrooms upstairs—

the main one opening onto a trellised Victorian veranda overlooking the tree-lined street below.

The whole place was furnished with modern furniture, but Scotty had brought in some eclectic pieces he couldn't live without. One of them was a black lacquered papier mâché, *bonheur du jour*, circa1840, which he had purchased as a birthday present for Mark during his last trip to London. This was a small and narrow day desk supported by spindly legs, beautifully inlaid with painted papier mâché, mother of pearl, tortoiseshell, and ivory—all forming an intricate Oriental design. I estimated the price for this piece would have been around ten thousand dollars. Another fine piece was an Italian ivory-lacquered side table from the 18th century with a dark green and yellow marble top, decorated with an elaborately carved frieze of scrolling foliage and flowers. This alone had cost him around fifty thousand dollars at auction in Sotheby's London.

I figured I was in a home with at least half a million dollars worth of antiques, just sitting around with a large marmalade cat as a guard. I smiled as I pictured Henry scurrying away inside the nearest wardrobe in the event burglars should break in.

My musing thoughts were interrupted by the little chime on my computer, signifying I had email. The message was from the dating site I was perusing, notifying me that someone had sent me a "Let's meet" request. I clicked on the link and it took me to the profile of my cyber-admirer, and I prepared myself to read another set of personal information.

The guy's name was Thomas. He was forty-two years of age, a civil engineer, divorced with two kids. He lived in the southern suburbs of Sydney and loved going to the movies, the beach and playing tennis. I scrolled further down on his profile page, but there wasn't much more information about him. His photo revealed an average-looking guy with brown hair, blue eyes, and a nice enough smile.

I looked up from the profile and sighed with disappointment. I knew what the problem was—I was comparing everyone to Josh, hence the reason I couldn't make up my mind about whom to date. Cheating aside, Josh was a good-looking man—tall, athletic build with handsome boyish looks, and a successful architect to boot. He loved fine dining, arts and culture, expensive cars, travelling to exotic destinations, and he was a sharp and stylish dresser. Josh had class.

Even so, that class hadn't stopped him from being a cheat. I looked back down at Thomas's profile and decided to click on the "Let's meet" request. After all, they all seemed to be Thomases this evening, and I didn't have the time or the heart to keep searching. I needed a date, and fast.

I sent my reply, giving him access to my email address so we could make arrangements to meet up for coffee, which brought my own dating dos and don'ts to mind. *Do* meet in a public place, preferably for coffee, so if things don't work out, you only have to finish your drink and move on. *Don't* let him pick you up from home. *Do* meet him at the venue and make sure you have your own transport.

Once done with my reply to Thomas, I decided to turn in for the night. Tomorrow was Friday and I had a long day ahead of me, running the store and then having to deliver the Moroccan tea set to Scotty's customer. Henry followed me to the bathroom and watched while I went through my getting-ready-for-bed routine. Then, he promptly jumped on the bed and nestled next to me after I pulled the quilt over my shoulders. It was still cold, but not enough for a heater. Besides, the purring mass of fluffiness next to me would keep me warm.

"Good night, Henry," I said and flipped off the light. I was rewarded with a soft meow and a little sandpaper tongue, licking the back of my hand.

The following day I was flat out at the shop, selling a number of items to Paddington's elite. Scotty was sure to be pleased. I offloaded five expensive items: a French provincial armoire; a shabby chic buffet hutch; a sterling silver Russian samovar, circa 1880; a Venetian crystal chandelier from early 1900; and a delicate English kneehole ladies' desk.

When I glanced at my watch, I was surprised, but pleased to see it was closing time. All I had to do now was deliver the Moroccan tea set, and then I could go home, order a pizza, and put up my feet. Scotty had a wonderful range of movie classics, and I was itching to watch *Casablanca* seeing as I was dealing with its owner—or at least, a real life restaurateur who had chosen to name his place after a fictitious character.

I locked the shop's front door and switched off the showroom lights before going to the small office in the back where I proceeded

11

to wrap the tea set with bubble wrap. The shop was quiet and I was already in down mode, and starting to relax, when the telephone on the rustic table we used as a desk shrilled loudly, making me jump. It was one of those 1930s black Bakelite phones with a high-pitched ring. I snatched up the receiver before the third ring, my heart still in my mouth.

"Good evening, Sheppard Antiques."

A rather deep timbered male voice spoke. "Scott Sheppard, please."

"I'm sorry, Mr Sheppard's not here," I informed the caller, and heard a sigh at the other end of the line.

"So where is he?" the caller uttered, his voice impatient.

His tone got my back up, and though I wanted to maintain my professionalism, I couldn't help myself when I firmly replied, "May I ask who's calling?"

There was a pause as if the caller was taken aback that I was challenging him. Then, I heard a click followed by silence, and I realised he hung up on me. How rude! I slammed down the receiver on its cradle and finished wrapping the tea set. I couldn't believe the nerve of some people.

Glancing at my watch, I hurried with my task. It was close to six now and my stomach grumbled with hunger. I'd only had a tiny sandwich at noon and didn't even get the chance to have a coffee during the day. The caller forgotten, I rummaged through my handbag to find Rick Blake's details and then left the shop through the back door, which led to a narrow alley where my Hyundai Getz hatchback was parked. I carefully deposited a number of packages containing various parts of the set in the back of the car and drove off to make my delivery.

Rick's Café was in trendy and very expensive Woollahra, so I had no doubt I was heading to an upmarket establishment. On the way, I wondered whether the tea set was for use in the restaurant or for its owner. Scotty hadn't had time to tell me much about the place, except the word "café" was simply adopted because of its theme, but in reality, the establishment was a renowned and well-frequented restaurant serving modern Australian cuisine fused with Moroccan and a touch of Asian.

I turned left into Queen Street from Oxford and drove along the main drag, which was flanked by specialty shops, trendy cafés, and expensive-looking restaurants. At this time of evening, there was absolutely no parking to be seen, so once I reached my destination I drove around the corner, hoping there would be parking for patrons behind the restaurant. Luckily, there was, and I managed to grab the last spot available. I parked the car and picked up the packages containing the expensive tea set. I knew it had cost close to five thousand dollars, so I had no doubt the piece was for the owner rather than for use in the restaurant.

Walking back up to the main street, I stopped in front of a whitewashed stucco building of Moroccan design with hand-worked timber window shutters and a heavy and intricately carved wooden double door for an entrance. A charcoal grey sign with white neon letters in an Arabic-looking font lit up the top of the entrance and read "Rick's Café".

I stepped inside the foyer with its ochre-coloured tiled flooring and glimpsed a high-ceilinged room with several arched exits leading to what looked like other, more intimate, dining alcoves. There were potted palms all around, casting mysterious shadows on the white walls; and from the ceiling, hung elaborately worked Moroccan brass lamps, shrouding the place in a muted golden light and giving it an atmosphere of intimacy.

Octagonal tile-topped tables with bentwood chairs were interspersed around the rooms, and some of the more intimate alcoves had plump cushions on which to sit for patrons who chose to dine Moroccan-style and sit on the floor. At one end of the main dining room, I espied a long, lacquered timber bar with shiny brass fittings and mirrored shelves on the wall, full of spirit and wine bottles; and directly in front of me was the maître d' greeting station, which consisted of a timber stand, beautifully worked in musharabi.

The place was virtually a recreation of the 1942 movie set of *Casablanca*, except this was a lot more sophisticated and, right now, buzzing with activity. Waiters wearing white shirts and pants with red cummerbunds whizzed by, holding brass trays high up above their heads, filled with dishes of food and drinks. There were diners at almost every table even though it was still early for dinner. Meanwhile, a trio of musicians in one of the alcoves was gathered around a baby grand piano, setting up their instruments in readiness for the evening's entertainment.

I noticed some of the patrons were simply having coffee and

cake, so it seemed Rick's was not only a quality restaurant, but also a venue for the discerning café-culture crowd.

"May I help you?" A tall, well-built black man wearing a white tuxedo jacket with black pants and bowtie addressed me.

I was still taking in the whole atmosphere of the place and felt myself transported back in time to the Morocco of WWII. At any moment now, I expected to see Humphrey Bogart moving toward me. Instead, I saw Hugh Jackman walking across the floor in my direction. My heart did a double somersault. This place really buzzed—even celebrities came here. What was Hugh Jackman doing, though, wearing a white tuxedo jacket with a red bowtie, similar in fashion to the one of the man who was standing in front of me?

"What's going on, Mohsen?" Hugh addressed the black man from a few feet away.

"Mr Blake, sir; I'm just trying to help this lady," Mohsen replied, and my jaw dropped.

I quickly readjusted my focus and realised the man walking toward me was not the actor, but Rick Blake, Scotty's client.

He stood facing me, and I closed my mouth. "How may I help you?" His voice had a familiar tone to it, and I experienced a moment of déjà vu.

There was a slight American accent in his rich, deep timbered... Oh, my God! It was the rude man who'd hung up on me less than half an hour ago. I was tongue-tied and wondering desperately how in hell I was going to get out of this one without being embarrassed.

I realised Rick Blake was waiting for an answer, and he had a faint look of impatience about him. I couldn't do anything to help the situation now; it was too late. Fortunately, I found my tongue. "I'm sorry," I uttered, clearing my throat as it threatened to shut down my vocal chords. "I'm from Sheppard's and I have your tea set." I nodded toward the packages in my arms and hoped I didn't drop anything breakable.

Rick Blake addressed his employee. "Mohsen, please take these packages to the office. I will look after the lady."

Great! He was going to give me a dressing down in private. Well, at least I wouldn't have to suffer the humiliation of being told off in front of another person. Mohsen took the packages from me and walked off while Rick Blake motioned for me to follow him.

We crossed the floor and headed toward the back of the bar to a

14

cosy booth, almost hidden from view of the public. The booth was shielded by a timber screen inlaid with mosaics, forming an arabesque design, and the seats were lined in deep red velvet. The timber tabletop was inlaid with mosaics similar to the screen, and there was a small brass lamp on top, casting an intimate glow. Rick Blake waited for me to take a seat and then sat opposite me.

"May I offer you something to drink?"

"A cappuccino will be fine, thank you." I momentarily lost myself in his smooth brown eyes and still couldn't get over his resemblance to the actor. Meanwhile, I was having a difficult time trying to maintain my composure. This Rick was nothing like the one in *Casablanca*. For starters, he wasn't in black and white—he was in full Technicolor and in 3D. Not only this, he did things to my body that I didn't care to analyse; and he hadn't even touched me! Don't even go there, I warned myself. When was the last time I'd had sex? 1912, my brain screamed back at me. I squirmed in my seat and tried to remain focused on the present.

Rick Blake ordered a cappuccino for me and an espresso for himself from the waiter who came to take the order; then, he turned to me with a dazzling smile. My knees felt weak.

"I guess you're the person I spoke with earlier on the phone." I nodded stupidly, and he went on, "I want to apologise for hanging up on you. We're having a record night tonight with a big function plus the regular crowd, and I'm short-staffed by three. So I guess you could say we're having a stressful night. This is the reason I was calling Scott. I wanted to tell him not to bother coming round until Monday."

"Oh." This was the only word that escaped from my lips, and I silently told myself to snap out of it.

"But where are my manners? I'm Rick Blake, the owner." He held out his hand toward me.

I shook it and felt his cool, firm grip, and I wished myself a hundred miles away from him. The last thing I wanted was for him to sense my desperate hormones, jumping up and down, and demanding a good shag.

"Cat Ryan," I managed to reply coolly. "I'm sorry about earlier." I smiled uneasily and almost jumped when a cappuccino appeared in front of me. "Thank you," I addressed the waiter who delivered it. I then turned back to my companion. "Mr Blake, I—"

15

"Rick. Please, call me Rick," he invited as he stirred sugar into his espresso.

"Rick, then." I savoured his name on my lips and took a sip of my drink to buy time in order to regain some kind of composure.

"Please, don't worry about the call. Just put it down to a misunderstanding." He threw me an easy smile, and my heart did a flip.

I had to get out of here fast. "Well, Rick," I spoke in between sips of coffee, wanting to finish the drink quickly so I could leave, "Scott's in Brisbane for a few days, and he asked me to deliver the tea set. I can see I'm keeping you from your busy evening, so I'd better go. Thank you for the coffee." Good call, I thought, praising myself on my newly found composure even though my legs still felt like jelly and my tongue stung from drinking hot coffee too quickly. I stood up, nonetheless, and held out my hand to him. He shook it.

"It was a pleasure meeting you, Miss Ryan." He stood with me. "I'll walk you out."

I prickled at his confident tone. How did he know I was a *Miss?* "Please, call me Cat," I invited graciously while all I wanted was to run out of the place and never lay eyes on him again.

We reached the front door. "Well, Cat, nice to meet you, and I hope to see you again if you drop by the café. Otherwise, I'll probably run into you at the shop. Scott tells me he has a new shipment coming in soon that may be of interest."

Right now, I could kill Scotty for doing this. He must have known the effect Rick Blake would have on me. I was sure this had all been a plan to throw me into Rick's path, hoping I would simply get over Josh in an instant.

"Yes, well… Until next time, I guess." I nodded politely, and almost winced when the band struck its first notes of "As Time Goes By". *Just my luck!* I left abruptly with Rick's eyes burning holes into my back.

Chapter 3

By the time I got back from Rick's, I was famished. Henry accosted me as soon as I walked in through the door and proceeded to tell me all about his day in a series of very loud meows, ending with a particularly squealing one, signifying I hadn't fed him yet and he wasn't too happy about it.

I dropped my shoulder bag on Scotty's sparkling white polyurethane and Caesar stone kitchen counter and went to the fridge to get the cat's kangaroo meat while trying not to trip over him as he padded in a figure-eight pattern between my legs.

"Henry! Be still," I scolded. He responded with an amber gleam that told me I had better get on with feeding him or else, and he pounced on the meat the moment I put it into his bowl. Then, I went straight to the phone and ordered a ham and pineapple pizza from Domino's. Not my first choice, but it was now close to eight, and I didn't have the inclination to go looking for a wood-fired pizza place around Paddington. Domino's was far quicker.

I changed from jeans and shirt into pyjamas before opening a can of Coke. Great diet, I thought, wrinkling my nose. I was sure this would all go straight to my waistline, but who cared? I intended to work it off during the weekend while enjoying jogging at Centennial Park; and it looked like we were in for sunny weather.

While I waited for the pizza to be delivered, I checked my emails. There was one from Scotty, telling me he had picked up a truckload of goodies from the estate sale and was now arranging to have the whole shipment delivered to the shop by next week. This'll keep me busy, I thought. There would be the whole process of unpacking, cleaning, cataloguing details in the stock register, and pricing. I was sure Scotty was going to ask me to work extra hours, which was great, except that I had to write my next blog post.

Another email notified me of a comment made on the blog. A woman wanted to know about dating etiquette when it came to paying on a first date. I wrote back, saying that in my opinion, if it was a matter of coffee, I would expect the man to pay, but if the date progressed to dinner, it would be better to go Dutch. This should eliminate the pressure on anyone who might feel obligated to the other person. If, however, the man asked the woman out on a second date, then he should pay. I opened this up as a topic for discussion because it was an interesting and sometimes touchy subject.

My third email was from Thomas, my potential date from the Let's Meet online-dating site. He wrote he would love to have coffee and was happy to meet me at *that great café in Woollahra*—Rick's Café. *Oh, no!* Of all the cafés in all the suburbs around Sydney, he had to pick this one. I smiled at the irony and very quickly typed back a reply, trying to dissuade him from meeting there.

I went on checking the rest of my emails, but Thomas happened to be online and contacted me through Yahoo chat. He said he particularly wanted to go to Rick's because he had heard so much about it, and would I mind? I sighed and gave in. What was one coffee, after all? I made arrangements to meet him there late Sunday afternoon, knowing I had to work first. I was glad that at least I had been able to find a date so I was going to have something to write about.

The pizza arrived when I was planning points to cover in my next blog post, and I put away the laptop and answered the door. After dinner, I tried to keep working. Henry cuddled up to me on the sofa and the rhythm of his tranquil purring made me relax, and I started to nod off. I had a busy day ahead of me at the shop tomorrow, and Sunday would be the same, so I picked up the cat and went to bed.

Saturday passed in a blur of customers asking a million questions about items, which resulted in sales for the shop. Sunday was a bit more sedate. I actually had time to have lunch and start working on my next blog post. I realised, though, that until I met up with

Thomas, I had nothing much to say. I groaned at the thought of my upcoming date. I was tired, and all I wanted to do was to go home and sleep, but the lure of earning such great money for writing a blog post was too much. I needed the extra income to build up my savings for that proverbial rainy day.

I closed the shop promptly at four, made myself presentable by applying make-up and lipstick, and with ten minutes left to spare, I rushed to Rick's to meet Thomas by half past the hour.

I was first to arrive and as I stood outside the place waiting, I thought it a good thing I'd arranged to meet Thomas out in the street because I didn't want to go into the café by myself in case I ran into its attractive owner. Ten minutes elapsed, and I started to pace up and down, hoping Thomas wasn't running late. He had my mobile number but hadn't called, so I figured he might be trying to find parking somewhere. Even on a Sunday, it was difficult to get a spot around busy Woollahra.

By quarter to five, I started to think Thomas had changed his mind about meeting me and hadn't bothered to call. Meanwhile, my legs felt tired from standing all day at the shop, and I was cold. Though the sun was still out, there was a chill wind blowing in from the nearby coast that cut through to the bone. I was practically salivating at the thought of a nice, hot cappuccino, and maybe even a blueberry muffin.

"Hi, sorry I'm late," a voice spoke from behind me, making me jump.

I turned and there was Thomas, standing up to his full height of five feet four inches, even though he'd stated on his profile that he was five-eight. *Hm!* Other than this, the only thing different from his profile was that he was balding, which wasn't the case in the photo he had posted on the site. This was a good point for my blog: beware of misleading information and old photographs. Good thing I wasn't really looking for someone; otherwise, I would have told the very unpunctual Thomas to take a hike.

"Did you get lost?" I queried, wishing he truly had got lost.

"No, it was the parking," he replied and extended a hand. "Anyway, I'm Thomas. Great to meet you."

I shook his hand and noticed his searching eyes had come to rest on my breasts. I cursed myself for having worn a T-shirt, especially as the chill wind made my nipples stand on end. I couldn't wait to go inside to get warm, and to run to the bathroom to wash my hands. Thomas's handshake reminded me of a wet fish.

"Likewise," I said and led the way in, no longer caring if Rick was about the place. Right now, I wanted to get the coffee over and done with so I could go home.

Mohsen, the maître d', was on duty, and after raising an eyebrow in surprise at seeing me again so soon, he led us to a quiet alcove instead of the open space of the main dining room.

"I'll have the waiter come to take your order," he announced as he handed us two menus.

Once he left, I dispensed with the menu and excused myself to go to the ladies' room. I asked Thomas to order me a cappuccino, and decided to forget about the muffin. I took a while in the ladies' until my nipples had time to defrost and in the meantime, I washed my hands twice before I went back out. By this time, my cappuccino was waiting.

"Sorry I took so long," I excused myself as I took the seat directly opposite him. "There was a bit of a line-up," I lied.

Thomas had ordered a macchiato for himself, and he was almost done with it. I stirred one sugar in my coffee and thanked God the lights in the alcove were dim; at least, my date couldn't keep ogling my breasts. I hated it when men did this. Instead of looking at your eyes when speaking, they spoke directly to your breasts. What a turnoff!

Thomas and I had nothing in common, as I found out within next ten minutes of inane chitchat. I was relieved when I finished my coffee and it was time to go. Then, to my horror, Thomas took out exactly three dollars from his wallet to pay for his coffee. I tried to keep a straight face. So much for my advice about letting the man pay! Still, I wasn't here to date for real, and so it didn't matter. In fact, without knowing, Thomas had made things easier for me. I paid for my coffee and prepared to leave immediately on the pretext that I had more work to do before I went home; and I felt no guilt at having brought our meeting to an end so abruptly, especially as he had turned out to be a skinflint.

Thomas told my breasts he was happy to have met me—*and them,* I added silently—and we would probably see each other online sometime.

I took this to mean he wasn't interested in me, only my boobs.

20

He probably worked out in his pea-brain that I wasn't impressed with him and, therefore, would not be seeing him again. I did everything I could to keep a smile on my face while resisting the urge to whack him one across the head. What a drip!

Quickly stepping out of the alcove with "boob-watcher boy" following behind, I almost collided with Rick—and to think I had been congratulating myself on having managed to evade him until now.

Rick put out two hands to steady me, and his touch on my bare arms sent such an infusion of heat surging through my body, I was taken aback and was sure I must be blushing like a virgin on her first date.

"Cat Ryan," he stated and smiled, showing white teeth against a tanned face.

My heart plummeted, and I wished I could disappear, especially as "boob-watcher boy" walked into me just as I collided into Rick. I pulled away and tried to recover my composure as quickly as possible by turning to Thomas and introducing him as "a friend". The men shook hands, and I wondered whether Rick was going to rush off to the bathroom to wash them as soon as he could get away from us.

"I have to go now," Thomas addressed me. *Thank God he didn't look at my boobs this time.* Then, he turned to Rick, "Nice to meet you, Rick. You have a great place here." These were his parting words before he disappeared through the main dining area and out the door.

I sighed with relief and noticed thankfully that Rick's eyes were on my face and not on my boobs. "Just a casual acquaintance who wanted to drop by your renowned establishment," I felt compelled to explain.

"And?" Rick asked with suppressed laughter in his warm brown eyes.

"And he loves the place, as you can see." I managed a smile. "It seems Rick's is well-known all over Sydney."

"We do enjoy a good reputation," he informed me. "It's nice to see you again, by the way. Friday was such a busy day I didn't even get a chance to chat with you for long. Do you have time for another coffee?"

The temptation was too much, but I needed to leave. The man was dangerous, and my heart was still in healing mode. The last thing I needed was an entanglement with the sexy Rick Blake. My body thought otherwise, however, which was the reason I had to remove myself from his magnetic presence.

"Perhaps some other time," I replied, "but thank you." He didn't say anything; he just regarded me as if trying to decide whether he had read me wrong. "Scotty's got a truckload of stuff coming through and I have to make room for it at the shop," I blabbed on, once again colouring under his gaze. "I'm sure he's going to call you next week and ask you to come over and have a look around. By the way, how did you like the tea set?" By steering the conversation to the subject of antiques, I felt more in control of my emotions.

"It's beautiful," Rick answered. "I'm remodelling one of the dining alcoves to resemble a Moroccan caravan, and I thought the tea set would set off the décor to perfection."

So he was going to use it in the restaurant, but not to serve patrons. "It's just right for that sort of thing. Do you often use real-life antiques for this purpose? I mean, aren't you afraid someone might break something?"

"We're insured," he replied. "Well, if I can't persuade you to have coffee, then I'd better get back to work."

The man is anything but subtle. This was a very direct signal that he was dismissing me. I wondered why he even took the trouble to invite me in the first place. It was obvious he wasn't interested in me sexually, and for all I knew, he was married with ten kids. I said, "Well, goodbye," and made to go out the door.

"I'll see you again sometime soon," he responded, sounding confident.

How dared he! "Perhaps," I threw over my shoulder as I left. The man had a nerve.

That night, Scotty arrived home just after ten, and the look on his face told me all was not well. When he walked in through the door, Henry jumped off the sofa where he had been nestling on my lap and regaled his owner with loud meows of welcome. I switched off the DVD I had been watching and took in Scotty's appearance: stunning blond and blue-eyed looks, smudged by dark circles of worry under the eyes.

"What's Mark done now?" I remarked before offering coffee, to which he nodded.

He bent down to pick up Henry and followed me into the kitchen where he sat at the shabby chic kitchen table and sighed. "We argued," he told me, his tone subdued.

"What about?" The fragrance of freshly roasted coffee beans made me think of Rick, but I quickly brought my mind back to Scotty and went on preparing the coffee in the Italian cappuccino maker.

"He's seeing someone else," Scotty announced, burying his face in Henry's fur.

"I'm sorry, Scotty," I uttered, patting his shoulder. "For what it's worth, I know how you feel." I sympathised with him; and it reminded me of Josh and the day I found out he had been cheating on me. I could still feel the pain like a knife cutting into my heart. It was obvious I was still smarting from the betrayal.

When I finished making the cappuccinos, I joined Scotty at the table. "Is this the first time he's done this?" I asked tentatively, not wanting to push him if he didn't want to talk.

"We've been through this once before," Scotty answered. He seemed glad to be able to confide in someone; and who better than a close friend? "We managed to get past it, but the trust is never there afterwards, you know?"

I nodded and waited for him to go on.

"Lately, I noticed he's become more distant, and every time he flies to London, he takes time out for a break. So I put two and two together and asked him if he was seeing someone else. He denied it. But then, a friend of ours ran into him over there. When I caught up with my friend last week, he told me he saw Mark being lovey-dovey with Eric." His mouth downturned and he regarded me with a look of pain in his eyes.

"I'm so sorry, Scotty."

"The worst part," Scotty continued, dropping the bombshell, "is that Eric is my ex."

I winced. Not *that* Eric! Eric had been Scotty's love for years, but the two broke up about a year ago when Mark came on the scene. Eric then moved to London to start afresh, and now he was supposedly Mark's lover. It suddenly occurred to me Eric might be on the rebound and using Mark to get back at Scotty.

A long sigh escaped from Scotty and he stood up. "Thanks for the coffee. I'm off to have a shower and then bed. I'm exhausted."

"Okay," I announced. "In that case, I'll go home."

"Stay over if you like. You're welcome company, plus Henry

23

likes to have his aunty around, too." This, at least, brought a smile to his face, and my heart warmed. It was so nice to feel needed.

After Josh, it was great to have family around me; and Scotty was my only family. I had lost both parents to illness within a few months of each other when I was in my twenties, and I had no other family in Australia. Apparently, I had a string of cousins in Italy and Ireland, but I never met any of them and didn't even know who they were. My parents had lived in a little world of their own, and when they passed on, they left me an orphan.

"I'd love to stay," I replied with a smile. "Come here and give me a hug goodnight."

We hugged for a long time, both deriving comfort from each other's touch. Then, Scotty turned in for the night while I cleaned up in the kitchen and afterwards went back to finish watching my movie.

I'm a glutton for punishment, I thought, as I switched the DVD back on and *Casablanca* appeared on the screen.

CHAPTER 4

Scotty's mood rubbed off on me and I went to bed thinking about Josh. The thought that he was now living with someone else had the power to hurt deeply even after almost a year.

I still couldn't understand what happened between us. We had gone out for about four years and then lived together for one, and all seemed well—except that unbeknownst to me, almost all the time we had been living under the same roof, Josh had been cheating on me.

I couldn't understand why this was the case. He had been kind and sweet during all our time together, though I had noticed of late our sexual activity had slowed down somewhat. Stupid me, put it down to the fact that since we were now living together, we no longer had the same urgent desire to make love; that we were so comfortable with one another the whole thing was a lot more relaxed.

I was convinced this happened to a certain extent once you settled into a relationship. So at first, I didn't know what was going on. No alarm bells went off in my head. Then, one day when Scotty returned from an auction, he told me he'd bumped into Josh and a young stunning-looking redhead. They had been having lunch at a café in Annandale and she seemed to be all over him. When Josh saw Scotty, he came up with the excuse that he was seeing off one of his co-workers who was leaving the firm. Scotty wasn't dumb, however, and he felt the energy between the two. So upon his return to the shop, he told me what was going on.

I might have been naïve enough to believe Josh had a "private" send off for a co-worker, except why have it in Annandale when Josh's firm was in Double Bay, all the way across town?

Elise was her name, and she was a junior partner at the firm. In desperation, I resorted to subterfuge by ringing the firm and asking for her; and sure enough, I was put through to her extension, but I hung up just as she answered. At first, I thought she hadn't yet left, but when I rang again a month later and she was still working there, I realised she wasn't leaving. It had all been a lie.

It took me a couple of months to confront Josh, and then it all came out. He had known Elise for a while and there was chemistry between them, though he tried to resist temptation—*how noble of him*—but alas, in the end, he had succumbed.

"So why stay quiet for a whole year?" I had asked, heartbroken. "Why not just tell me and be done with it?"

His answer was even more hurtful than finding out he had been unfaithful. Elise was in a complicated relationship and until she was sure she could make the break, she and Josh had decided to keep it a secret. *How considerate of her.* So I assumed if I hadn't found out about them, they would still be carrying on behind my back until Elise was good and ready to move on from her other relationship.

At the time, I'd felt so debased, so used, that right there and then, I packed my bags and left Josh without a word. I had gone straight to Scotty's and he took me in, no questions asked, until I found a place for myself.

Shortly thereafter, I heard through an acquaintance who worked with Josh that he and Elise were engaged to be married. Talk about having your heart cut out! What a bastard Josh had turned out to be. I would've had more respect for him had he told me straight out that he wanted a break up. There had been no need to go skulking behind my back to have an interoffice affair, making sure all was in place before he moved on.

I tossed and turned in bed with my head full of Josh and then decided this wasn't getting me anywhere. The clock on the bedside table showed it was just past midnight. I might as well get up and do something productive; so I went to my computer. Work was a wonderful antidote for a broken heart.

26

Cat Ryan's Dating Blog #2

First date disaster! I met up with T (Please note: only initials will be used to protect the innocent—and the not-so-innocent).

Date broke rule number one—he was late, and I had to stand out in the cold, waiting for at least twenty minutes.

Date broke rule number two—he paid for his coffee and left me to pay for mine. As for the rest, I won't even bore you with the details.

So let's talk first-meeting etiquette. To date, I've had 114 comments for the man paying for coffee on the first meeting and 3 comments against. For the ladies who voted against—don't you think we're taking women's lib a bit too far? After all, what's one coffee? I would buy this much for any homeless person I meet in the street, let alone a potential friend or someone who might become more intimate.

My point? If the man wants to meet you, he can at least buy you a coffee. If he doesn't, I would take this as a sign that he's going to be a lot more stringent with his money later. You are, of course, welcome to disagree, but to put it bluntly, I don't think any of you want to end up with a tightarse.

In regards to the lateness—well, let's put it this way, if he's going to be late for a first date and doesn't even bother to ring, how is he going to behave on your wedding day?

Questions are invited on the above points.

Dating Q&As

Q: I've been on two dates now. The first time, he forgot his wallet at home; the second, he didn't have time to go to the ATM. What you do you think?
Jenna, New South Wales.

A: Jenna, I have one word for you—RUN!

Q: My date was a good-looking guy; and he paid for our coffees and cake. He was also punctual and very charming throughout our meeting. The only thing I'm puzzled about is that he's only available to meet with me on certain

27

weeknights, namely between the hours of 6.00pm to 8.00pm. He says he has a lot of work on and is usually very tired afterwards. Also, weekends are a busy time for him because this is when he catches up with the work he didn't get done over the week. What do you think?

Emma, Queensland.

A: Emma, there are two possibilities as far as I'm concerned:

1. He's a male prostitute and needs late nights for business, and days to sleep it off, OR

2. He's married, and 6.00pm to 8.00pm on certain nights are the times when he tells his poor, deluded wife he's "off to the gym". My advice, as with Jenna's from New South Wales, is RUN!

There were a lot more questions on the post, but I decided to deal with them the following day. Just thinking about these bloody men who were late, cheapskates, or cheaters was enough to exhaust me.

I shut off the computer and went back to bed, feeling more relaxed. And just when I was about to fall asleep, an image popped into my head—the image of Rick Blake. Suddenly, my body felt alive and I wondered how I could feel like this when I was still nursing a broken heart. Perhaps, my mind was trying to shut out the pain with the idea of mindless sex. The man exuded raw male sexual power, and I knew I didn't have a chance if he got me alone in a room.

"Down, boys!" I told my raging hormones, wondering why I thought they were male instead of female. Why not "Down, girls"? I didn't know the answer to this question and right now, it was too late for me to lie awake trying to analyse it. I needed my sleep. Tomorrow, I had the day off and I was going to use it to hunt around for my second date.

I had forty-seven "Let's meet" requests and spent most of the day culling through them. It was obvious my profile photo was drawing them in.

I had posted a picture taken by one of the magazine's photographers. Needless to say, he did a great job of airbrushing away the ravages of age—though he swore he hadn't touched up the photo at all. It was kind of him to say this, but I didn't believe him.

For starters, when I was under stress or didn't get enough sleep,

I got puffy eyes; and on the day before my photo shoot, I distinctly remember having had a good cry about Josh. Then, there was the matter of crow's feet. Scotty kept telling me I was so lucky to have inherited my Mediterranean skin from my mother; but let's face it, he was biased and trying to comfort a dear friend.

It never occurred to me at the time that I was probably being overly critical about my looks, as was the case with most women in modern society. We were, after all, competing with twelve-year-old models who had velvety skin and a dewy look, and who were made up to look eighteen. You just couldn't get away from this look of youthful innocence when you flipped through any women's magazines—including the one for which I worked. And let's not even get into the "waif look", either! These days, the skinnier the woman, the sexier she was considered to be. At least, I was slim and blessed with generous breasts, which of course would have been frowned upon on the catwalk scene; but I had never yet come across a man who complained about their size.

I turned my thoughts back to the requests in front of me and as I scanned through each profile it struck me how none of the men requesting a meeting had actually read a word I'd written on my profile. Yet, most of them had the hide to say they were not superficial and that personality counted the most in their ideal partner. *Yeah, right!*

I had stated I was looking for a male, somewhere between thirty-eight to forty-five years of age, minimum height of five-eight, slim to average in size, and a non-smoker who loved animals, travel, and had a taste for culture.

A vast majority of the men who requested to meet me were over forty-five; some of them quite chubby, and definitely under five-eight. There were twenty-five smokers, and only ten of them liked animals. There was nothing about culture in their profiles, but a lot about sports, especially rugby. *Ugh!* Slim pickings; not to mention their obviously short attention spans.

After a second look through the profiles, I finally settled on three possibles that came as close as I was ever going to get to the criteria I'd set down. I replied to them.

The rest of the day, I spent cleaning my small studio apartment and doing the groceries. Scotty telephoned in the afternoon.

"Do you want to work tomorrow? I've got the first shipment

29

coming in from the Brisbane estate sale and we need to go through and catalogue everything."

"Sure," I replied, glad of the extra work. "How are you feeling today, by the way?"

He paused as if trying to gather his composure before he declared, "I'm holding it together."

"Did you hear from Mark?" I asked while hoping he would simply disappear from the face of the earth and leave Scotty alone to heal. Mark was a real bitch, I thought uncharitably.

"No. But I don't expect him to call any time soon." Scotty sounded forlorn. "He'll leave it for a couple of weeks and then he'll call apologising and promising it was simply temptation, and that he won't do it again."

I cried with indignation, "And you're going to forgive him one more time I suppose."

Scotty didn't answer straight away; his silence said it all. He would allow himself to be suckered in by Mark yet again.

"Anyway," I continued, changing the subject in order to save him further heartache, "I may have three possible dates coming up, so I'll have something to write about in my next blog post."

We talked a little about my online dating experience and some of the requests I had received, and then we rang off. After dinner, I checked my emails and found two of the three possibles had replied. They both wanted to meet mid-week in the evening, and since I knew I would be working at the shop during the weekend, I didn't mind. The only problem was each man nominated Wednesday as his preferred day for the meeting. I had to write my blog by Thursday, so I decided to squeeze them both in on the same evening—five-thirty and six-thirty respectively.

In order to do this, I had to meet them somewhere close by so I could go straight from the shop to the meeting. I also needed to meet them at the same venue in order to stick to my time deadline. But where to go? I thought for a moment, and the answer came to me in an instant—Rick's Café. With those private dining alcoves, it was the perfect venue. I could meet the first guy in one alcove; then swap to another for my second meeting, and none would be the wiser. The other aspect I liked about the café was that I could park in the patrons' parking area, which made me feel safer. After all, who knew what these guys would turn out to be like? If one of them was a nutcase, at least I would be within screaming range of the staff. Then, the tall Mohsen or his athletic-looking boss could rush to my aid.

The only downside to using Rick's as a venue was that I might run into its owner—and what would he think of me, turning up with a different man all the time? *It doesn't matter what he thinks of me. What matters is I'll feel safe while I work on this gig, and I won't be tempted to fantasise about Rick Blake if I'm with another man. Good plan!*

Before I had time to think further about this, I responded to the requests and proposed the times and the venue for the meetings. An agreement from each man arrived before bedtime.

CHAPTER 5

I arrived at Rick's ten minutes early in the hope I could get a nice, private alcove for my meeting with Brian, my five-thirty. God, it felt like I was interviewing people for a job: Brian, my five-thirty, and Peter, my six-thirty.

I smirked, conjuring up an image of me, sitting in an office with a waiting room full of men, filling out application forms. Then, one by one, I called them in for their interview. "So tell me," I would say from one side of a massive walnut desk, "what kind of a dater are you, and why do you think you should be selected to go out with me?" Shaking my head at the ridiculousness of this, I looked around the café in search of a place to sit, hoping Rick wouldn't appear and wonder what I was doing there.

"Can I help you, miss?"

I jumped, whirled around, and sighed with relief when I came face to face with a short, mustachioed waiter wearing white pants and shirt set off by a red fez on his black curly-haired head. "Oh, I'm meeting someone for coffee and was hoping to find somewhere quiet to sit. Business, you know," I remarked casually as if I did this all the time.

"How about one of our alcoves?" Red Fez suggested.

I threw him a dazzling smile. "Thank you, that'll be perfect. Do you have one from where I can see the front door?" I queried, thinking ahead to my meeting with Brian. I wanted to be able to spot him and wave at him from my position so I wouldn't have to go down to meet him in the main foyer and run the risk of being spotted by Rick.

Red Fez led the way to an alcove located to the right of the main dining area and found me a seat at a table behind a potted palm tree. Very discreet, but with a direct view of the main foyer. Perfect. I thanked him and placed in his hand a five-dollar tip for his trouble.

At first, he refused to take it, but upon my insistence, he pocketed the money and thanked me profusely as he offered me something to drink. I asked for a cappuccino and settled down to wait for Brian.

At five-thirty on the dot, a slender man of average height with mousy brown hair walked into the foyer. Brian looked just like his photo. I made a mental note for my next blog—one point for being punctual and another for posting a recent photo of himself so I could recognise him straight away.

I leaned over the alcove's open archway and waved. He saw me and made his way toward me, and I smiled at how easy my private alcove plan had been as I prepared to greet my first date for the evening.

"Hi, I'm Brian." He introduced himself cheerily when he reached me.

We didn't shake hands but merely smiled at each other. "I'm Cat," I replied.

Just then, Red Fez came by with my cappuccino and took Brian's order for a skinny latte. Meanwhile, I reminded myself that I could only be with Brian until quarter past six. Then, I would have to find a way to get rid of him before Peter arrived.

"This is a nice place," Brian observed when Red Fez walked off to fetch his order. "Is this a regular hangout for you?"

I opened my mouth to reply, but he went on without pausing for my response.

"Well of course, it must be. Look at this place; it's great. You know, I've lived in the area for a long time and didn't even know this place existed. So what do you do?"

Again, I opened my mouth to tell him, but he didn't wait for me to speak.

"I work at a local radio station, reading the news and introducing music from new bands. You know, there's such great talent out there—some really great, young musos trying to make it big on the scene. It's tough for them, though; and I'd like to think I give them a chance to feature their work..." And on and on he talked as my eyes glazed over.

I thought it would be a nice thing if he gave me the chance to get a word in edgewise, but this was not to be. Brian talked nonstop from the minute he arrived and through three skinny lattes without asking if I wanted another coffee. He even ignored Red Fez when he came over to ask if I wanted anything else. Good thing I didn't because I was saving myself for a second cappuccino with my six-thirty.

Nodding at Brian while he kept up with the verbal diarrhea, I glanced down at my watch—ten to six. I threw a few furtive looks toward the main dining room in case Rick Blake should make an appearance and was glad that up until now, he hadn't. I then drained the rest of my coffee and tried to stay focused on what my companion was saying. It was impossible. He had gone from talking about his radio show to his owning a holiday cabin at some beach, which was four hours out of Sydney and backed onto a national park full of kangaroos, and then he remarked how great it would be if I came out to visit there.

In his dreams! I raised one eyebrow ever so slightly, but of course, he didn't notice—he just kept talking. Now, he was going on about home cooking versus eating out, especially as prices in restaurants were skyrocketing all over Sydney. Another glance at my watch, and I almost jumped out of my chair. It was quarter past six, and Brian showed no sign of ending his monologue any time soon. I had to do something, and very quickly.

"Oh," I interrupted him mid-sentence as he was complaining about the increasing traffic problems in the city. "Will you excuse me? Nature calls." I escaped before he had a chance to respond.

In the toilet, I dialled Scotty from my mobile.

"Cat," he responded, obviously seeing my name on the caller ID. "I thought you were out on a date."

"A date from hell," I declared, glancing at my watch once again. Six-twenty! "Look, I have to make this quick. Call me in exactly sixty seconds and tell me I'm needed at the shop for inventory."

"What—" he started to say, but I didn't let him finish.

"Don't ask. I don't have time to explain. Just do it!" I hung up, hurried out of the toilet, and smashed into what seemed to be a brick wall, one that smelled of a wonderful, woody aftershave. Two arms reached out to steady me, and I was suddenly face to face with Rick.

"What is going—" he began, but I interrupted.

"Oh, hi, Rick. Have to dash. Sorry about bumping into you. I wasn't watching where I was going." I didn't give him a chance to say anything else before escaping from his enquiring gaze.

As soon as I reached the alcove and sat down, Brian continued from where he had left off. "I think the state government should do something about the traffic jams, don't you? They keep reporting in the news they're looking into it, but they've been saying this for the last ten years. It's really annoying how—"

My mobile started to ring. I threw him an apologetic look. "It's my boss. Excuse me, but I have to take this." I hit the answer button, and Scotty repeated exactly what I had asked him to say earlier. "I'm just in Woollahra," I spoke into the phone, "so I can be there in ten minutes. Is that okay with you?" Pause. "Fine, I'll see you soon." I hung up, and for once Brian was silent, waiting for me to explain.

I hoped my eyes conveyed a look of regret when I stated, "I'm so sorry, Brian, but I have to go. My boss needs me for stock inventory, and I forgot all about it."

Brian didn't look too convinced. "Inventory?" he queried. "What kind of job do you do?"

"Well, it's a shame I didn't get a chance to tell you," I threw at him, hoping he got the message that he had hoarded all our time together because he was in love with the sound of his own voice. "Anyway, I really have to go now. So goodbye."

Brian stood and I squeezed past his chair. "What about meeting up again? I think we really connected."

"I'll email you," I told him, hoping my mouth didn't gape open in amazement at his nerve. "Bye."

I made my way out of the alcove and across the main dining room toward the exit. Rick was watching me from the bar, but I pretended not to see him and walked out of the café. Once out, I ran across the road and took cover inside Chez Chocolat, a Belgian chocolate shop. While pretending to browse through the many trays of handmade chocolates on display at the window, I espied Brian coming out of the café and walking down the street. I waited for a couple of minutes to make sure he was out of sight before I went back into Rick's. The time was six-thirty on the dot, and for once I hoped my date would be late.

I was not disappointed. Peter was running about fifteen minutes late due to heavy traffic, but at least he called on the mobile. This gave me time to go inside and find another quiet alcove before the dinner crowd started to arrive.

The alcove I shared earlier with Brian would have been perfect, but I chose one on the other side of the main dining room. The last thing I needed was for Brian to walk back in for some reason, find me at the café with another man, and know I had lied. It was bad enough I was dating because of my blog and not because I was truly looking. Having said this, if I happened to meet someone nice, it would be a bonus.

My new alcove was just as discreet as the other one, but I didn't have a clear view of the front foyer, so when Peter arrived, I didn't see him. He called from his mobile to let me know he was standing at the entrance, and I went out front to meet him, but not before I was spotted by Rick again, who was still behind the bar serving patrons. They were obviously short-staffed once more, I thought gratefully; so Rick was too busy to come over to see what I was up to.

This time, as I walked past the bar to go to the foyer, I waved to him from a distance. He waved back, looking rather mystified at my comings and goings.

Peter stood by the maître'd station. He was short, chubby, and balding. If he hadn't raised a hand in greeting when he saw me, I would never have recognised him. His photo had depicted a man of solid build—not chubby—with a full head of hair, and he had listed his height at five-nine, though to me, he looked more like five-six. I knew this because I was five-four and he was only slightly taller than I.

Peter shook my hand with a firm grip, and I led him back to the alcove, wondering why I was putting myself through this. Perhaps, the five hundred dollars I was getting for each blog post wasn't worth it after all.

We walked past the bar and I felt Rick's gaze on me. He was probably wondering what in blazes I was up to, but luckily, he was still very busy and wasn't able to approach me. Once seated in the alcove, Red Fez came to take our order. Thankfully, he kept quiet and didn't say something such as "Nice to see you twice this evening." This would have made matters a little embarrassing.

I ordered another cappuccino, and Peter asked for hot chocolate. After Red Fez left to fill our order, I became aware that

Peter's eyes had been on me from the time we ordered our drinks. He was probably sizing me up, but I didn't care for his intense gaze. There was something a little strange about his pale blue eyes. I squirmed in my seat while trying to look at ease.

"So, it's nice to meet you, Peter," I remarked, and for some reason decided not to mention the fact that I didn't appreciate his posting a photo that was probably taken ten years ago. I had the feeling Peter knew what I was thinking, and the hair at the back of my neck stood on end. I decided to give myself half an hour max with this guy; then, I would leave on the pretext that I was meeting friends for dinner.

"Sorry about the lateness," Peter apologised, but somehow he didn't sound as sincere as he had earlier when he'd called from his car. "The traffic was rather heavy, and I came all the way from Mt Druitt."

Mt Druitt? That was miles away on the other side of Sydney. I was surprised he'd even agreed to meet me in Woollahra. He must've been sitting in traffic for a good hour or more—and this was on a good day.

"That's quite a drive," I declared, softening toward him and deciding that I was reading too much into this feeling of mine. The guy had to be a decent type; otherwise, he would never have made the effort to come so far. His next words, however, made me rethink the whole thing.

"It was worth the drive to meet you," he uttered, and his eyes moved from my mouth to my breasts and back again.

I cleared my throat and wished myself anywhere but here, especially when he ran the tip of his tongue along his thin lower lip. Oh, my God! He was leering at me. Fortunately, Red Fez came to the rescue with our drinks, and this gave me time to compose myself. *Just drink your coffee as quickly as possible, Cat; and then tell him you've got to cut it short because you have a dinner engagement.* Searching for something to say, I remarked, "I read on your profile that you're an accountant."

"Yes," he answered, slurping on his hot chocolate, the noise making me feel queasy. It was like he was snorting it rather than drinking it. "That's what I do, but I hate it. There are some days when I feel I could just freak out, you know. Remember that movie with Michael Douglas called *Falling Down*?"

Suddenly, I felt sick to my stomach and my heart started

thumping inside my head. Meanwhile, his eyes hadn't left my face—or rather, my mouth—and he didn't blink even once. I quickly glanced at his eyes and noticed his eyelashes were so fine it was as if he didn't have any. The words "serial killer" appeared on the screen of my mind, and I had to use my full willpower to stay seated opposite him, sipping my coffee like we were old friends.

Peter's gaze was almost a blank stare. He talked at either my mouth or my breasts, and sometimes alternated quickly between the two. He was a talker like Brian, but this time, I was grateful. I didn't want to divulge too much about myself.

He asked what I did for a living. I lied and told him I worked at an auction house. In my profile, I had written I worked with antiques; therefore, saying I worked at an auction house was consistent with the information I posted even though it wasn't entirely true. Peter didn't really try to find out much more about me, though. He simply talked about his life, namely the fact that he had never been married and lived in a house with two Rottweilers he'd named Acid and Trip.

"Nice." I threw him a nervous smile.

"You know, it gets lonely sometimes being in the singles' game," Peter went on with his story. "I used to live with my mother until she passed on, and then I stayed in the same house. I don't have any other family, you see." He paused for a moment to lick his lower lip again. "The problem in living with your mother, though, is you can never bring girls home."

I nodded faintly and kept sipping my coffee as an image of Norman Bates popped into my mind, and I felt sickened at the thought that Peter may have done away with his old lady.

His eyes once again took in my breasts, and he went on talking. "It's hard to have sex when your mother is in the next room." This time, his voice got a little breathy, and I hoped it was because he had a problem with ingesting dairy and was developing phlegm, rather than because he was getting excited at the thought of sex—possibly with me. *Oh, help!*

I took a large gulp of my coffee so I could finish it fast, but the drink was too hot and it burned its way down my esophagus.

"So what about you?" Peter asked as if finally realising he hadn't given me a chance to talk. "Do you like to do it with someone else in the room next to yours?"

"I... I..." I was speechless as I tried to work out whether I had heard correctly. "I beg...your pardon?" I managed to utter.

Peter sighed and slurped the last of his hot chocolate. "I asked if you like to live with someone in the room next to yours."

"Oh." Relief coursed through my body. *Get a grip, Cat!* "Ah, no. I..." I was going to tell him I lived alone, but then changed my mind just in time. "What I meant to say is my flatmate's a quiet man, and half the time I don't even know he's in the house."

Peter's blank stare was back on my mouth. "Well then, you're lucky. So how about another cup of coffee?" He nodded toward my almost empty cup.

"Oh, um, oh... You know, I actually have a dinner engagement. It's a shame you were running late," I pointed out as if I regretted it, "and we're not able to have more time. Unfortunately, I have to go."

He stood up. "No problem," he stated, reaching for his wallet. "Let me go and settle this and I'll walk you to your car."

"No need to do that, Peter," I interjected quickly. "I'm just out the back."

"It's not a problem. I always escort a lady to her car."

His thin smile gave me the creeps, and I fleetingly wondered whether he whacked the lady over the head and killed her right there and then or he took her out bush and threw her body in a creek after he had his way with her. I had to do something fast before this weirdo latched onto me.

Peter went down to the bar to settle the bill, and an idea of how I was going to make my escape came to me.

Chapter 6

"Hugh!" I called out loudly enough for Peter to hear and walked toward Rick Blake, who was in his shirtsleeves and just coming out of his private booth at the end of the bar.

Rick looked at me as though I had grown an extra arm and stood rooted to the spot with an enquiring expression on his face. I sailed up to him as fast as my legs would carry me and gave him a big hug and kiss on the cheek.

"Play along," I managed to whisper in his ear.

He was very quick on the uptake, and before I knew it, he was holding me against his firm body and kissing me on one cheek, then the other, European style. I almost swooned when I breathed in his sexy aftershave.

Peter regarded us with his creepy eyes, but this time I didn't feel spooked. "Oh, how rude of me," I declared in a cheery voice. "Peter, this is Hugh, a dear friend of mine."

The men shook hands while I stayed in the circle of Rick's arms, not because I loved the feel of his touch, but because he hadn't released me. "Remember I said I had to go for dinner with friends?" I reminded Peter. "Hugh is joining me."

Peter nodded, his pale eyes boring into mine. "Well then, I guess this is goodbye," he stated in a firm voice. "Take care." He then turned to Rick, nodded a goodbye, and left the café.

I must've slumped against Rick with relief and before I knew it, I found myself sitting in his private booth with him seated opposite me. He motioned for the barman to bring us a cognac and turned his attention me. "Care to explain what's going on with you tonight?"

40

I panicked momentarily while still trying to recover from the effects of his touch and the lingering aroma of his aftershave, now impregnated in my clothes. Rick was waiting for an answer, but I managed to buy a few more precious seconds as the barman came over with our drinks and a small brass bowl filled with almonds and dates. I was suddenly starving and eyed them longingly.

"Help yourself," Rick invited with a smile and sipped his cognac. I was grateful he was giving me a chance to recover and popped an almond in my mouth.

Rick waited quietly until I ate a date and two more almonds, and had a few sips of the wonderful French cognac. The liquid burned its way down my throat and I started to feel more in control—the episode with Peter almost forgotten. "I apologise. You must think I'm crazy." I smiled, feeling rather uncomfortable. I still didn't know what I was going to say by way of explanation.

"Who was that guy, and why did you call me 'Hugh'?" Rick looked mildly amused. Perhaps, he was enjoying my discomfort. I felt like walking out without an explanation, but I couldn't do this to my rescuer.

I explained with sudden inspiration, "Peter's a client who wanted me to hunt down a Georgian hall table, but I think he believed I came along with the goodies. He was coming on to me, and I had to get rid of him."

Rick didn't look too convinced but accepted my explanation with a knowing smile. I hoped he didn't see right through me. "What about the 'Hugh' bit?"

"Oh, that. I couldn't very well call you by your real name, could I? Peter would've put two and two together and known you're the owner of this place and not an old friend."

"Who says I can't be an old friend *and* the owner of this place at the same time?" he shot back at me with a raised eyebrow. "And why not Bob or Joe? Why Hugh?"

Good question. One I was unfortunately going to have to answer, and at the same time sound like an idiot. "Well, for starters, you don't look like a Bob or a Joe, and... um... and..." I couldn't say it.

"And?" he prompted with that knowing smile again, and I wanted to disappear into thin air.

"All right then!" I sighed with resignation and confessed, "When I first met you, I thought you looked like Hugh Jackman, the actor. I

41

guess the name stuck." There, I hoped he was happy. He looked smug for a moment, and I wanted to throw a date at his head.

He must've read my thoughts because he remarked, "Those are for eating, and you look positively starving. So let me buy you dinner. It's almost seven-thirty."

I was totally disarmed. The man had a talent for making me lose my composure, get annoyed with him, be grateful to him, and at the same time, charm me until all I wanted was to throw myself back into his strong arms and beg him to ravish me.

"Dinner would be lovely, thank you," I heard myself reply and was convinced the Cat Ryan I knew was having an out-of-body experience and someone else was inside.

Rick took charge and ordered Moroccan-spiced roast poussin served with wild rice, a side dish of lightly steamed vegetables mixed with apricots and almonds, and minted couscous.

"This'll be quite filling," he stated as the waiter who took the order walked away, "but if you want an entrée, let me suggest something."

"That's fine. It sounds like a feast already, and I don't think I can eat a whole chicken, either," I declared.

"The poussin is small, and we only serve a half bird. You'll be able to manage it."

I smiled. "Sounds delicious."

Rick ordered a fruity white wine from the Barossa Valley to go with the meal, and while we waited for the food to arrive, I relaxed in his company. The man was so attractive he made my hormones go into overdrive, but he exuded such a stimulating persona while he talked that I became curious about him as a person and forgot all about my sex-starved existence for a time.

He asked me about my job at Scotty's, and we talked about our mutual love of antiques. He seemed quite knowledgeable and it was wonderful to sip the cool white wine and be with someone who shared my passion.

"How long have you worked with antiques?" he asked after we finished discussing the French influence in English furniture.

"Since I met Scotty years ago and he offered me a job at his shop," I answered. "I've loved antiques, though, ever since I can remember. I particularly love anything to do with the Renaissance period, especially the paintings."

42

"Have you been to Tuscany?"

"Yes, when I was much younger. But I hope to go again one day soon. I'm writing a book on Renaissance art and the trip will be part of my research. The job at Scotty's is my bread and butter," I explained while at the same time I thought of Josh and his empty promises of a trip to Tuscany for our first anniversary living together.

I must've frowned at this thought because Rick said, "Is something the matter?"

I smiled reassuringly. "Not really. I was just thinking about wasted time—you know, putting your plans on hold for a person when all the while you could have carried on with your life if you hadn't waited."

Rick looked at me thoughtfully as he refilled our wine glasses. "Are we talking about a relationship gone wrong now?"

I nodded. "Something like that. But hey, let's not waste time on the past." I didn't want to think about Josh right now.

Rick smiled, and the whiteness of his teeth stood in stark contrast to his tanned face. My stomach did a flip and I looked down at my drink. I didn't want him to read the hunger in my eyes, and I wasn't thinking about food.

"What about you? I detect an American accent." I knew he was from New York because Scotty had told me, but I didn't want Rick to know that I knew.

"New York born and bred," he replied. "I came to live here with my Australian wife and when we broke up, I stayed on."

So he had been married. I was dying to know all the details, but I didn't think it would be appropriate to ask on our first date—and this wasn't even a date, only a chance encounter because he'd gotten me out of a sticky situation. "You must like Sydney, then," I commented, and decided if he wanted to volunteer information about himself, he would in his own good time.

"I love the weather here, plus the fresh produce," he stated and then laughed at my puzzled look. "I meant the food. I'm a qualified chef and I used to run a well-known restaurant back in New York City. Getting fresh produce over there was not always that easy, and most times we had to import out of season produce for the dishes we offered. Over here, it's a lot easier. Besides, once my business became more established in Sydney, I didn't want to pack up and leave."

"You don't miss your family?" I thought this a safe enough

43

question to ask.

"My parents are both gone and my only sister is married with three kids. She lives in Vermont. I visit her every couple of years or so. What about you, do you have family?" He turned the conversation around.

"No. I also lost my parents and unlike you, I was an only child," I replied with something like sadness in my voice, but to my relief, the food arrived. I really didn't want to talk about my orphan-like existence. "Wow, this looks great," I exclaimed as I took in the dishes, which were served in multi-coloured ceramic tagines. Our plates were made of brass with intricately carved patterns, as was our cutlery. "I'm relieved you're not going to make me eat with my fingers," I uttered in jest.

Rick laughed. "You'd be surprised at the number of patrons who actually want to do just that, but it can get quite messy."

The waiter placed half a poussin on my plate and served it with fragrant wild rice. He then lifted the lid off a serving tagine and the smell of freshly steamed vegetables with almonds, apricots, and faint spices made my mouth water. I nodded yes to his enquiring look, and after serving me, he asked if I wanted couscous. The minty aroma of the fluffy couscous created a wonderful cooling contrast to the other spicy dishes. I said yes to the couscous as well, and noticed Rick's pleased smile. He obviously liked his women to have a healthy appetite—but I wasn't one of his women. What was the matter with me?

Rick told the waiter he would serve himself and the man bowed slightly and walked off. "Dig in," he invited. "Enjoy."

I did enjoy. The flavours were a blend of sweet, spicy, and cooling, and everything I ate melted in my mouth. I had never had Moroccan food before, and I loved it.

During the meal, we went back to talking about antiques and my book. Rick listened attentively with genuine interest, but then he turned the conversation to the earlier events of the evening.

"Before Peter, I saw you with another guy. Was he also a client?" he remarked casually.

I hated to have to lie, but I didn't want him to know about the blogging gig and my dating under false pretences. For some reason, I didn't want him to think less of me; and if I told him about my dating arrangements, I had a feeling he would disapprove.

"Yes," I replied. "Sometimes clients want us to scout for particular pieces—just as Scotty did for you with the tea set."

"But why meet them here instead of the shop? You seemed frightened by Peter, so why not let Scott deal with him?"

He had a point, and I was going to have to keep lying. Oh, what a tangled web we weave when first we practise to deceive! I thought about Sir Walter Scott's quote and mentally prepared to deliver another lie.

"These clients are mine, you see, and I feel safer with them in a public place such as this café rather than the privacy of the shop. Scotty isn't always around, so I'd rather deal with male clients this way."

Surprisingly, Rick accepted my explanation. After all, it sounded like common sense. "In that case, feel free to come here any time," he offered. "At least, I can keep an eye on you." His smile did things to my heart that I didn't care to analyse.

"Thank you," I uttered, quickly changing the subject. "Mmm. This has got to be the best food I've ever tasted."

"Wait till dessert," he declared. "I thought we'd finish with sticky date pudding even though it's not strictly Moroccan. I have some wonderful King Island cream that'll knock your socks off."

We laughed at his comment. "I love King Island cream," I stated. "In fact, I love anything that comes from King Island. It's just so fresh."

"I told you I loved the fresh produce of this country," he remarked, and we laughed again.

We shared the sticky date pudding in butterscotch sauce with King Island cream on the side and drank espressos. I was stuffed by the time we finished and felt totally relaxed. It was early, only about nine, and music from the live band playing in one of the alcoves filtered down to us. The music was mainly swing with a touch of jazz.

"So why the 'Rick's Café' theme, aside from the fact your name resembles that of the character in the movie?"

Rick's dark eyes looked even darker in the subdued lighting of the restaurant and once again, my hormones tried to get the better of me, but I managed to quell my rising desire.

"I spent some time in Morocco during my travels years ago and loved it. So when I decided to run my own place in New York, I recreated Rick's Café, like in the movie. It was a good business, but I sold the place when I came to live in Sydney. Years later, when I was planning to open my own place again I decided to go for the same theme."

"Well, judging from the dining crowd, you certainly made the right decision," I commented.

"Yes," he agreed, "and I'm proud to say we've been voted one of the top five restaurants in Sydney for the fifth year running." He wasn't boasting when he said this; it was just a simple statement, suggesting the café's reputation was backed by a lot of hard work.

I made a mental note to read up about the place on the internet. It might reveal a lot more about its owner in addition to what I had learned so far. In the meantime, I realised I had taken up enough of his time, and if they were truly short-staffed this evening, as I had thought earlier, then Rick would be itching to get back to work.

"Well, it certainly has my vote," I said and stood up. Rick stood with me. "Thank you, Rick, for the lovely dinner. I really enjoyed it, but I've taken up enough of your time so I should get going."

He didn't try to persuade me to stay, which disappointed me even though I was aware the man was busy. He walked with me out the door and around the corner to the patron's car park.

"Be sure to stay safe." He watched as I unlocked my car door. "And remember you're welcome to bring your clients here. Next time, let me know in advance and I'll reserve an alcove for you."

I felt guilty. Cat Ryan, you're a big liar, I chastised myself. "Thank you," I replied. "Goodnight."

He reached for my hand and kissed the back of it, sending a little thrill of desire coursing through my veins. "Until we meet again."

I got into my car before I fell down in front of him and made a fool of myself, and managed to nonchalantly wave goodbye as I drove off.

CHAPTER 7

Cat Ryan's Dating Blog #3

With a few more dates behind me, I want to emphasise the concept of safety. Below are some points for consideration:

1. Always, and I mean ALWAYS, meet in a public place. A café is perfect because it usually has people in it even if it's only the staff, plus it's an enclosed place—so if you have to scream for some reason, someone is sure to hear you. You may think a park is equally public and safe, but if it's a large park, sometimes there is no one within "screaming range." Then, what will you do if he drags you behind a big tree or into a deserted skateboarding bowl?

2. Carry a mobile phone at all times and ensure the battery is full. If you need to call someone to your aid because your date is giving you the heebie-jeebies or simply boring you so much that you need a friend to give you a "rescue call" at least you can rest assured in the knowledge that the mobile won't cut out on you. This brings up another point: make sure you are in an area with a good reception signal.

3. Park your car somewhere that is well lit and close by, and never let your date escort you to your car. No matter how well you think you got along during your meeting, remember you don't know him well enough, and it's better to be safe than to be confronted by the Belanglo Forest serial killer.

4. Let a friend or family member know you are internet dating, and leave details with them such as the name and contact number of the person you are about to meet. This way, if you are not home by a certain time, the police will have

47

something to go on with when they are trying to locate you.

5. Finally, don't let anyone know where you live or work—and certainly never give them your surname or home telephone number. As for emails, it's always best if you use a web-based account such as Gmail or Hotmail. This way, if you get a stalker, you can always abandon the account and open a new one.

Dating Q&As

Q: My date looked really sexy in his photo, and sounded sexy on the phone. We talked for hours by phone and really seemed to hit it off. So when I finally met him face to face, I couldn't believe it was the same guy. He was almost like a total stranger, and if it hadn't been for his voice, I would never have recognised him.

Disappointed, South Australia

A: Hello, Disappointed, and welcome to the club. One of my date's photos must've fallen through a time warp and landed ten years later on the internet dating site. The solid build had turned to chubbiness; the full head of hair was something from yesteryear; and in the process of ageing, I reckon he shrunk by several inches in height. Luckily, I had my trusty mobile with me so I slipped into the toilets and asked a friend to give me a "rescue call". It worked beautifully. (This answer was based on a mixture of my last two dates—Brian, the one who talked his head off and had me running to the loo to ask Scotty for a rescue call; and Peter, whose photo had fallen through a time warp. My readers wouldn't know this, but I could still impart my dating wisdom).

Q: Do you think guys get their photos airbrushed? My date was really cute in his photo and looked like Johnny Depp. In person, he looked more like the headless horseman in The Legend of Sleepy Hollow. LOL.

Anne, New South Wales

A: Hi Anne, please read what I wrote for Disappointed and you will realise that at some stage or other we are all in the same boat. Good luck with your ongoing search, and stay away from headless horsemen.

The blog had a long list of questions and comments, and I spent a couple of hours answering them plus responding to others that had

48

been left from the previous blog post. We now had a consensus on the question of the man paying for coffee at the first meeting—there was resounding agreement that he should.

I got up from my desk and stretched. It was close to midnight and I had been at the computer since my return home from dinner with Rick. My hormones settled after a strong cup of chamomile tea and though I still felt Rick's kiss on the back of my hand, I could no longer feel the spot burning from the imprint of his lips. I wondered if he felt the same way about me after the time I kissed him on the cheek when pretending his name was Hugh. Somehow, I didn't think he would be daydreaming about me right now; more than likely, he was still at the café attending to business.

The telephone rang, making me jump out of my skin. For an instant I thought Peter, the serial killer, had somehow managed to get a hold of my landline number and was calling to see if I had *"checked the children"*. Knowing I was being irrational, I quickly swept up the receiver, wondering if perhaps it was Rick. I was, after all, listed in the white pages.

"Sorry to call so late," Scotty said when I picked up.

"Is something wrong?" I asked, feeling concerned. Even Scotty didn't ring this late at night.

"I wondered whether you'd like to come over and stay with me and Henry for a few days."

"What happened with Mark?" I knew this would be the only reason he would ring at this hour.

"I weakened and called him. He's in London again, and Eric answered the phone so I hung up." He sounded depressed. "Will you come and stay with me?"

"Of course I'll come. I'll be there tomorrow," I reassured him, feeling protective. He was like a brother to me, and I hated it that Mark was treating him like dirt. If only Scotty would find the strength to break off the relationship for good. "Do you want me at the shop tomorrow?" I added, remembering he had an auction to attend.

"Yes," he stated, already sounding in better spirits. "Come tomorrow and bring your things. I'll cook for us in the evening and we'll watch some of my movie classics."

I loved it when Scotty cooked for me. It was like going to a top-notch restaurant. Not only was he a gourmet cook, but he took care of all the little details—even down to the flowers and candles on the table. He was a romantic at heart and always went to a lot of trouble, even for a friend. On top of this, after one of his wonderful dinners, he wouldn't let me lift a finger. Plus, once he cleaned up, he would cuddle up with me on the big suede sofa, with Henry sitting on his lap, and we watched a golden oldie. Why didn't God make straight men in this way?

Scotty asked me how my dates had gone, and I told him about the self-centred Brian and the creepy Peter, followed by my rescue. He perked up at this and was suddenly very interested in what had transpired during my dinner with Rick.

"Nothing," I told him. I certainly wasn't going to admit to Scotty that the man had a way of making me forget propriety by wanting to drop my knickers and jump into his bed. Therefore, I brought the conversation to a close by saying I was tired and wanted to get some sleep. Scotty let me go even though he declared I was simply using this as an excuse not to talk about the gorgeous café owner.

I rang off so I wouldn't have to answer him and before bed, I went back online to google *Rick's Café*. The search results didn't tell me much more about him that I didn't already know, except that he had been running the café for close to ten years and the place was always winning some award or other. There was also mention that although Rick was a qualified chef, he had traded in his chef's hat for a host's tuxedo while still making all the operational decisions, inclusive of menu design.

Reading through the café's website, plus several articles written by food critics and journalists, I found out Rick's café in New York City had been a big hit and Rick had sold it for several million dollars when he came to live in Australia. Other than this, there was nothing about his personal history, and not one single mention of an Australian wife.

I yawned and realised it was close to one in the morning. I would pack for my stay at Scotty's prior to going to work. Right now, I needed sleep. I shut down the laptop and went to get ready for bed.

The next few days kept me busy at the shop with customers or with cataloguing the pieces Scotty had brought in through the many estate sales he had gone to and the auctions he had attended.

In the evenings, Scotty cooked a sumptuous meal of some kind, and we sat out on the terrace, overlooking his wonderfully landscaped garden, and ate by candlelight with Henry rubbing himself against our legs or simply lying stretched out on the cool sandstone floor, fast asleep.

We were now having a "Charlton Heston fest", and so far, we watched *Ben Hur*, *The Ten Commandments*, and *The Agony and the Ecstasy*. Tonight, we were going to watch *The Naked Jungle*. Meanwhile, I hardly spent any time online. Tomorrow was Thursday and I had nothing to write about although I had heaps of questions and comments to reply to. I decided that after the movie I would try to set up a date with someone—anyone.

"By the way," I informed Scotty while I helped him clear up the dishes even though he didn't want me to. "You need to know I'm taking all my internet dates to Rick's."

Scotty raised one brow in curiosity but allowed me to continue uninterrupted.

"I feel safe there," I explained. "But I told Rick these guys are clients who want me to scout for pieces." I cleared my throat when I saw the look he threw at me. "You disapprove?" I asked, already knowing the answer.

"Why not tell him the truth? It's not like you're his girlfriend, and there's no real harm in what you're doing. Rick's is a good venue for you, and you said you feel safe there. Besides, you're doing a writing assignment, not prostituting yourself."

I gave him an agonised look. "I know. It's just that he caught me unawares with the Peter thing and all, and I didn't know what to say. I didn't want him to think I was an incurable flirt or something worse."

"Cat," Scotty pointed out, "how can you be a flirt when all you're doing is a blogging gig? It's like research, darling."

He was right, of course. Yet, there was still something I didn't like about the way in which I approached the whole thing—dating under false pretences, as I had called it earlier. I didn't feel comfortable explaining this to Rick—not when I was beginning to get to know him. I didn't want him to think badly of me in any way.

"Scotty, I really don't see any harm in keeping this from him. It's my business, after all; and I only have another couple of months of doing this gig. Then, the whole assignment will be over."

His eyes held a doubting look. "You said if you got loads of hits, there was a chance the assignment would be extended."

"You're right," I concurred, taking my time arranging plates and

51

glasses into the dishwasher so I could avoid his gaze, "but somehow I don't think it'll come to that. There's only so much one can say about internet dating. The rest is just Q&As and comments left by the readers. I can look after those without having to go out on pretend dates."

Scotty grabbed hold of my wrist before I could force more items into the washer. "You know what I think?" I waited for him to go on. "I think you don't want Rick to know about all this because you find him attractive, and you want to go out with him."

I pulled my arm away as if I had been scalded with hot water. "That's not true! I'm still getting over Josh, you know. I'm not ready for real dating."

Scotty laughed. "Come on, darling. This is me you're talking to. You may still be getting over that good-for-nothing Josh, but you've got the hots for Rick really bad."

I blushed, and he smiled with delight.

"Rick's a really nice guy, and he's single," he stated. "So why don't you go for him?"

"How do you know he's single?" I arched a brow at him in doubt.

"He was voted one of the top ten eligible bachelors on the Sydney scene in last month's Marie Claire."

I didn't even ask why Scotty was looking through women's magazines, but then again, he would be interested in the bachelors for himself.

"Scotty," I uttered, repressing impatience, "the guy may be single, but this doesn't mean he's celibate. He may even have a girlfriend or two stashed away somewhere."

"You could be right, but I don't think he'd be serious about any of them now that he met you."

In his own way, Scotty was as much a charmer as Rick Blake. If he wasn't gay, I would have married him in a jiffy. I gave him a hug and kissed his cheek. "You always know how to make a woman feel special. What a shame you're a gay boy."

He threw me a cheeky smile. "I can also make gay boys feel special."

I laughed and ruffled his hair. "Why don't you finish up here while I set up the movie?"

We finished watching the movie at around eleven, and Scotty

went straight to bed while I went online to search through my "Let's meet" requests. I was tired and needed sleep, but my blog post was due and I had to find another date.

Henry came to help me look for someone, so he sat on my lap and groomed his "pink bits" while I scanned through the fifty or so profiles I received in the last couple of days.

There were so many different characteristics and personality types, I really couldn't make heads or tails out of my culling process. In the end, I made up a table on Word with three columns, entitling them *Losers, Maybes*, and *Will Dos*. I didn't have a definite *Yes* column as this could only come after I met the guy and had a chance to see what he was like.

"Loser, loser, maybe, loser, loser... maybe, loser... " I was talking aloud and Henry glanced at me and then went back to doing his bits. "Will Do!" I finally exclaimed after more than an hour sifting through losers and maybes. Henry was asleep on my lap but woke up and threw me a dirty look. I ignored him.

My "Will Do" man was named Robert. He was quite good looking, in a rugged sort of way, with brown hair and blue eyes. He'd made a point of stating that his photo was taken only a month before, and this earned him brownie points in my estimation.

He was six-foot two, slender but sporty, non-smoker, divorced with no kids, and a freelance photographer for several well-known magazines. Jackpot! I thought excitedly. Could it be that Rob, as he called himself, was the one? Well, at least a promising contender for my blog post, I reminded myself seeing as I wasn't out there to date for real. Still, if I met the right guy, I might just give it a go. I certainly had nothing to lose.

What about Rick? The thought popped in my head. But I wasn't dating him. Besides, he was far too dangerous. I knew I could fall in love with the man, and I was sure he would end up breaking my heart. Isn't that what irresistible men always do?

I'd had my fair share of "bad boys" in life, and they all ended up hurting me somehow or other. As far as I was concerned, Rick fell under the "bad boy" category; so as exciting and gorgeous as he was, I'd learned my lesson, and bad boys were banned forever.

I emailed Rob, telling him I was available for a meeting on Thursday evening at Rick's Café; then shooed Henry out of my bedroom and went to bed.

53

Next morning, when I was getting ready for work, I checked my emails. Rob had confirmed. I was excited about this one and looking forward to our meeting. It would be great to have something positive to write about in my blog. Perhaps, there was hope for internet daters after all.

CHAPTER 8

I decided to dress up for my date with Rob. Usually, I went straight from the shop to Rick's wearing jeans and a shirt, but this evening I made the effort to look more presentable. I wore a long flowing skirt of dark green with a snowy white Indian cotton blouse. I then accessorised with a wide, antique brass bracelet, intricately carved with a Middle Eastern motif and peppered with small green stones resembling emeralds; a pair of dangling earrings and a pendant on a hand worked chain went with it. The overall effect was a little Moroccan in style, and I thought I would blend in well at Rick's.

As was my habit, I wore little make-up, only using a small amount of compressed powder, mascara, and reddish lipstick. My hair looked a bit spiky after the trim I had the week before at my hairdresser's and it gave me a pixie-like appearance. I loved it—it took at least five years off my face.

Rick wasn't around when I arrived, and I was thankful. Mohsen, who was on duty, showed me to the alcove I'd had once before where I could see the foyer through the potted palm tree.

"Miss Ryan," he addressed me, and I was surprised he remembered my name. "Mr Rick said if you should come in I'm to give you this alcove at all times. Would you like something to drink?"

I was impressed, and excited that I was finally going to be able to brag about having "my usual" both in terms of where I sat at the café and what I had to drink. "A cappuccino, please." I gave Mohsen a dazzling smile, and he bowed and left with my order.

This was marvellous! I was now a regular at Rick's, and as the band started to play some soft swing music, I felt like I was in one of the movie classics I usually watched with Scotty.

Rob arrived promptly at six o'clock, and I waved to him from the alcove. He joined me just as Mohsen personally brought my cappuccino. I felt I was getting the royal treatment tonight and nothing could go wrong. When Mohsen asked Rob what he would like to drink, he ordered a latte.

"Wow, you look great! Your photo doesn't do you justice," Rob exclaimed with an admiring look in his eyes. This earned him another point in my estimation.

I had come up with a Man Eligibility Scale, and figured if a man earned five points on it, I would date him again. Eight points, and I'd let him kiss me. Ten points, and I'd marry him and have his child.

My Man Eligibility Scale went thus:

1. Must have a recent photo on his profile
2. Must tell the truth about his looks, career, marital status, etc
3. Must be punctual at all times or telephone if running late
4. Must pick up the tab on the first date
5. Must have nice manners and be charming
6. Must be a good listener
7. Must be sensitive and caring
8. Must always tell the truth about his past
9. Must be looking for a long-term relationship with a view to marriage
10. Must be open-minded about having children.

Bonus points were given for being a non-smoker, a sensible drinker (if he drank alcohol), and having a love of animals.

All points, however, would be revoked immediately if the guy turned out to be a slob, had a drinking or drug problem, was unhygienic, used bad language, tried to come on to me too soon or broke any of the Man Eligibility Scale criteria. Reminding myself to post this on my blog, I turned a big smile on Rob.

"Thank you, Rob. Lovely to meet you," I replied, all graciousness.

We chitchatted about the weather, the traffic, and other general topics until Rob's latte arrived, and then we conversed about more personal things.

"So how long have you been on 'Let's Meet'?" I asked him.

"This is only my second date," he answered, sounding a little shy.

My heart warmed to him immediately. "Well, if it's any consolation, I'm fairly new to this, too."

"So how are you finding it? Met anyone interesting yet?"

"If I had, I wouldn't be here now, would I?" I remarked, trying to catch him out.

This was one thing to which I hadn't given much thought. What happened if you met someone you liked? Did you take your profile off the site right away? I had heard that certain men went on looking even after they met someone they were seeing regularly. It was as if they wanted to keep all their options open, obviously not serious enough about making a commitment.

This had happened to one of the readers on my blog. She had been seeing this guy for at least three months, and they had moved their relationship to the bedroom. Then, one day, she caught him browsing on the site.

He had changed his username and tweaked his age and some other personal details so she wouldn't find him out, but he had used the same photo. Although she'd taken her own profile down, she received an email from the site, notifying her of new profiles—and sure enough, there he was.

The other alternative would have been for him to hide his picture, but guys who did this never received as many hits. I always warned women on the blog never to go for someone who hid their picture or says he'd send one if a woman got in touch with him. My theory was if you have nothing to hide, you should publish your picture on the site for the entire world to see.

Rob gazed at me thoughtfully. "Well, it's nice to know you didn't meet anybody just yet—it means I have a chance."

Hm. Another brownie point for being charming. "And how about you? How was your first meeting?"

Unfortunately, my question opened the floodgates and Rob went on to tell me about the first woman he met, who turned out to be a drug user. She had met up with him to try to exchange sex for money in order to buy drugs.

I cringed but didn't offer any comment; the reason, like one of my earlier dates, was that he didn't give me a chance to speak. He

57

simply went on and on about how they should ban people like this woman from the site, and how this wasted his time when he didn't have any to waste, what with his very busy job and trying to get over a break up with his wife of fifteen years.

I didn't want to form an opinion about him just yet, so I put down his verbose manner to the fact he had been through a major break up and perhaps needed to talk and get the whole thing out of his system. What I didn't figure on, however, was that two cappuccinos later, and three more lattes for Rob, he had gone on to tell me all about the intimate details of the break up with his wife.

I learned he caught her cheating with someone from work—I could relate to this one, and maybe this is why I let him carry on— then, there had been a long period in the relationship where it was on and off until she finally told him it was over for good. At this point, Rob told me about the wonderful years they had spent together and how he could not understand why she'd left him.

Didn't fifteen years mean anything to her? He questioned passionately, on the verge of tears. I didn't know the answer to this so I kept nodding sympathetically and let him continue. At one point, he had to stop talking because he broke into sobs, and I was so embarrassed I excused myself and went to the ladies'.

I noticed it was around seven-thirty and I had been sitting there, listening to a heartbroken man, for the last hour and a half. If he had tried the same thing on his other date then, I didn't blame the woman for going on drugs. In a moment of dark humour, it occurred to me there was a chance she wasn't really a druggie, but was driven to drugs by Rob.

On my way out of the ladies', I bumped into Rick. Smirking, he declared, "You must be a bad businesswoman."

I didn't know what he was talking about and threw him a puzzled look.

He smiled charmingly and explained, "You reduced your client to tears." He nodded toward Rob, who was busy wiping at his eyes with a napkin.

I rolled my eyes, but before I could tell Rick to buzz off, he disarmed me by kissing my cheek and saying, "When you're done, join me for a drink." Then, he walked off.

I looked up at Rob and despite my wobbly legs after Rick's kiss, I walked across the main dining room and up the few steps leading to the alcove, determined to put an end to this disastrous date. I resolved Rob was going to lose all his points for being a crybaby.

"Rob, I'm sorry about your break up. I really feel for you because I recently came off a break up myself," I commiserated with him when I reached the table and sat back down. "But the thing is we go on the dating site in order to meet new people. And it seems to me, you're not ready to move on. How long has it been since you broke up?"

"Two years," sniffed Rob.

Two years! And he was still crying? She must've really done a number on him. "Rob," I said, wanting to give the poor man some comfort, but at the same time send him on his way so I could get out of here and grab some dinner. Three cappuccinos on an empty stomach didn't sit well, and I was beginning to feel the effects of it. "Rob," I said again, "you're a nice man and have a lot going for you. I'm sure when you can put this behind you life will turn around and you might meet the right person. In the meantime, take a page from your own book and don't meet with anyone until you're truly ready. Right now, you're wasting not only your time, but the other person's."

As I delivered my advice, I felt like a real phony. I was doing exactly the same thing, but for a different reason. I was wasting people's time as a result of my research for a blog on dating—except they didn't know it. *Oh, Cat, this gig is not as easy as you thought it would be.*

"Of course, you're right," Rob agreed. He reached across the table and kissed me lightly on the cheek. "Thank you, Cat. I'm going to seek some counselling and try to move on. I'm sorry about dumping on you like this. You're a wonderful person to listen to me so patiently."

I felt guilty, but there was nothing I could do. "Good luck with everything, Rob. I wish you all the best." I went to reach for my wallet; after all, I only expected the guy to pay for one cappuccino, not three, but Rob wouldn't let me pay. After a sniffly goodbye, he left me at the alcove and went to settle the bill before he left the café.

I felt exhausted after Rob's emotional outpouring and just wanted to go home. Rick had invited me for a drink, but I was too tired to socialise right now, so I picked up my bag in preparation to make a move when from the corner of my eye I saw two figures and froze.

I dropped my bag on the floor and hid behind the palm tree as I espied Josh entering the main dining room with his arm around Elise. At least, I assumed it was Elise from the description Scotty had given me when he had bumped into them.

From my vantage point, I was able to see them clearly. Josh looked his usual handsome self, and Elise was a slim redhead with supermodel looks. It wasn't the looks that caught my attention, however, or the little black dress she was wearing that clung to her body like a second skin—it was the huge rock she wore on her ring finger. I had never in my life seen such a large diamond; and suddenly, unexpectedly, I broke into tears and felt just like Rob.

I knew Josh was going to marry. I was told this by an acquaintance who worked with him, but what I couldn't accept was that Josh spent years without committing to me, until the last year of our relationship—and this had only been to live together. With Elise, on the other hand, it took him less than twelve months, and he was already engaged to be married to her. How did this happen? I obviously hadn't meant much to him. A sob rose to my throat and I escaped to the ladies' before Josh had a chance to see me.

I managed to pull myself together although my eyes were still blotchy from the crying. The only thought in my mind right now was to get out of the café, but I didn't want to chance bumping into Josh. Before I ran into the toilet, I saw them heading in my direction, toward one of the private alcoves. This meant I wouldn't be able to go out through the main dining room—Josh was bound to see me. My only alternative was to sneak through the kitchen and out the back. I knew from previous visits that the kitchen opened onto the delivery dock and the patrons' car park.

Peeking through the partially opened toilet door, I managed to see where Josh was seated with Elise. His alcove gave onto the main dining area so if I walked out in the open, I would definitely be spotted.

No guts, no glory, I thought as I came out of the toilets, made a right turn, and headed toward the bar and the kitchen beyond. A hand snaked out and grabbed hold of my wrist just as I was sneaking past the private booth behind the bar. Rick pulled me into the booth as my eyes looked longingly at the swinging kitchen door. So close!

Rick noticed my red eyes despite the subdued lighting in the booth. He had been having his dinner, and perhaps had seen the whole thing. I was beginning to think the man had eyes in the back of his head. He confirmed this when he declared, "So not only do you make your clients cry, but you cry in sympathy with them."

I wrinkled my nose and threw him a look of annoyance. "I have to go, and I didn't know you were voted in as the policeman for the evening," I replied sarcastically.

"Whoa, methinks the lady doth protest too much," he remarked with a lurking smile about his lips that I itched to slap away. "Listen, I don't know what's going on with you and your clients, but I think I'm entitled to ask why you're making people cry in my restaurant. I don't want patrons thinking it's the food."

His eyes held a glint of genuine amusement, and I smiled even though I was still annoyed with him. "Very well."

"Good." He relaxed back in his seat and motioned for one of the waiters. "Let me get you something to eat. You must be starving."

I lost my appetite after seeing Josh and his ladylove, but I had to eat something after having drunk all that coffee. My stomach was making gurgling noises, which wasn't good—and it was bad enough I probably resembled a panda since I hadn't been totally successful in wiping off all of the mascara that had run with my tears. So I nodded and allowed Rick to order for me.

"You don't mind if I finish my dinner?" He asked as the waiter disappeared into the kitchen. "In the meantime, can I offer you some wine?"

"No, thanks." I shook my head. "I think some cool water would be better."

Before I could say I was happy to go to the bar and order it for myself, Rick left the booth and quickly returned with a bottle of Pellegrino. "Thank you," I said when he poured me a glass.

"Now, tell me what's going on." He regarded me with sympathy in his eyes, and I felt the tears coming back.

Oh no! I couldn't possibly cry in front of him. I threw another longing look toward the kitchen door and wished I could escape. When I turned back, it was to find a hand holding out a paper napkin to me. I took it and dabbed at my eyes.

"Take your time. I'm here for you whenever you're ready." Rick resumed eating his dinner and left me in peace.

I appreciated his sensitivity and decided to award him a point from my Man Eligibility Scale even though he wasn't a date. Meanwhile, I sat quietly until my dinner arrived and was surprised to find I still had an appetite after all. The couscous with lamb in yoghurt sauce was too delicious to waste.

Rick watched me with amusement in his eyes as I downed the meal. I didn't mind. He remained silent and ordered an espresso once he finished his dinner. I felt better with every bite I took. Finally, when I finished eating and sat back, looking relaxed, Rick spoke.

"Okay, so care to tell me what's going on?"

I hesitated for a moment, but then decided to confide in him. He had proven to be the perfect companion during a crisis, taking control and giving me time to regain my composure, so he deserved an explanation.

"See the couple who walked in about fifteen minutes ago and is now sitting in the alcove nearest the band?"

Rick looked out of the booth for a moment. "The one with the good looking redhead?"

Trust him to notice Elise; but then she was a stunning woman. "Yes, that's the one. Well, the man with her is my ex. We broke up almost a year ago and he's now engaged to Elise—that's the redhead's name. The worst part is while I was still with Josh, he was cheating on me with her, and I wouldn't have found out if Scotty hadn't bumped into them."

Rick gazed at me thoughtfully. "I see," he stated without further comment.

I felt irritated all of a sudden. "Is that all you're going to say?"

"What else do you want me to say? You obviously broke it off once you found out about her, and that's the end."

I revised my opinion of him and decided I wasn't going to give him a point for sensitivity. He was, after all, like any other good looking man—insensitive and a womaniser. He was indeed one of the bad boys. I pursed my lips at the thought and saw him smile from the corner of my eye.

"You think this is amusing?" I snapped.

"Not at all. It's just that I can't understand women sometimes. You broke up with him, right?"

I nodded.

"Okay, so why keep the flame alive? He's moved on, and so should you. Why break into tears because you see him with another woman? You knew he was going to marry her. You just said so."

I sighed, annoyed at him. "Just because I broke it off doesn't mean I don't have any feelings for him. He broke my heart, you know!"

He regarded me with concern in his eyes. "Listen to me, Cat. Don't waste your time on someone who doesn't deserve you. Okay, so he broke your heart—all the more reason to move on and forget about him. You obviously don't want to settle for someone who's going to cheat on you, so don't waste any time or energy on him. Would you take him back if he came crawling to you?"

I shook my head.

"Right," uttered Rick, "then move on, and live your life."

"How can you do that?" I exclaimed.

"Do what?" He sounded surprised.

"How can you be so practical and dismissive of the whole thing? Don't you have any feelings?" I really wanted to slap his face. He was being a typical, insensitive male.

"In matters of a broken heart, it pays to be pragmatic," he replied, his voice hardening a little. "You've already let him hurt you once, so why let him hurt you again by carrying a torch around for him?"

Much as I hated to admit it, he had a point. It was bad enough I'd allowed Josh to hurt me, so why go on letting him hurt me even more? I had the power to put a stop to this by simply focusing on a future where I was better off without him—a future where one day I might meet the right person. I had just given this same advice to Rob, so now I should take heed of it and do as I had told him; let it go. Put the past behind me and release the old to make room for the new. Suddenly, I felt lighter of spirit and I had Rick to thank for it.

Scotty had tried to tell me the same thing, but because he was a dear friend, I chose to wallow in self-pity instead, knowing no matter which way I went, he would be there to comfort me. With Rick, though, it was different. He made me see the situation in the cold light of day through the eyes of someone who was neutral. I had a sneaking suspicion his wisdom came from the experience with his own marriage break up. I didn't know anything about the circumstances, but perhaps she had been cheating on him, too— although I couldn't imagine why any woman would want to cheat on Rick. He was the epitome of the perfect man, I decided—a bad boy reformed.

"Thank you," I uttered. "Sometimes it takes a stranger to put things into perspective."

"Why are you calling me a stranger? I thought by now we were at least friends," he remarked.

I suspected he was trying to flirt with me. "Very well. Thank you, *friend*," I replied, and picked up my bag. "And now, I must go."

"So soon?" He threw me a smile that weakened my knees. Oh, he was good at this game.

"Yes, I have to work tomorrow. Thank you for dinner. It was delicious, and though I feel much better about the Josh thing, if you don't mind, I'd still like to leave through your kitchen." This time, I threw him a smile; a wicked one.

"Very well, but let me see you out." He stood and motioned for me to follow.

We walked through the busy kitchen, and I noticed some curious glances from the chefs and kitchen hands, but I didn't care what they thought; let them draw their own conclusions.

It was dark out and Rick grabbed hold of my arm to guide me through the bumpy, gravelled car park. Once we reached my car, he let go, and I inexplicably missed his touch.

"Well, goodnight," I said and went to unlock my car door.

"What do you say to a picnic on Sunday?" Rick suggested, catching me by surprise.

He was asking me out, and I didn't know what to say. Of course I wanted to go out with him, but at the same time, I didn't want to break my own rule and go out with a bad boy. But hadn't I just decided he was a bad boy reformed?

"Well?" Rick prompted when he saw me frown in thought. "We're friends, remember?"

Trust him to say something like this and make it impossible for me to refuse. "Okay," I accepted. "I'd like that, but first I have to check with Scotty in case he wants me to work on Sunday."

"Give me a call," he stated and drew out a business card from his pocket. "This is my mobile number."

I took the card and put it in my bag. "I'll let you know tomorrow." I turned to go, but he stopped me by taking hold of my arm again.

"By the way, why *was* that man crying earlier?" This time, he was

64

genuinely curious.

I smiled and answered, "Even clients suffer from broken hearts."

CHAPTER 9

When I told him about Rick's invitation, Scotty wouldn't hear of my working on Sunday, and he started to plan what I should wear.

I had been hoping he would want me to work, but it seemed he was more intent on promoting a relationship between Rick and me; and although I showed faint disapproval at his eagerness to get me married off—or at least to get me a new boyfriend—I was secretly delighted I had his stamp of approval. I reminded myself a bad boy reformed was not in the true sense a "bad boy" and, therefore, not on my list of no-nos. So in the end, I allowed myself to be swept along by Scotty's eagerness.

"You can't wear jeans, darling!" Scotty reproved me with shock in his eyes when I made the suggestion that jeans and a shirt would do. "If I know anything about Rick, this is going to be a romantic picnic, so you can't show up like you've just come from the shop after a hard day's work." He paused and regarded me intently for a few moments, making me think I had spinach stuck between my two front teeth or worse, a big red zit right in the middle of my forehead. "I see white," Scotty announced, hands on hips.

"White?" I repeated like a simpleton.

I had no idea what he was talking about, but knowing him, this was going to be a huge production. Even Henry got in on the act, walking into the room and gazing at me with a calculating eye.

"You're in luck," Scotty declared with excitement. "In last week's estate sale, I bought some wonderful vintage clothing—"

I baulked. "I'm not going to wear some dead person's clothes.

66

You're mad!"

"Hush, dear," he chided, unfazed by my outburst. "Stay here and I'll be right back." He made for the door; then paused, turning to address me from the doorway. "Oh, and strip."

"Strip? What—"

"Just do as I say," he ordered and disappeared.

I looked down at Henry, who was now curled up on my bed and cleaning in between his front toes. "The man's lost it, Henry. Did you hear? Your master is a sandwich short of a picnic, if you'll pardon the pun."

Henry looked up at the mention of his name but lost interest very quickly in what I had to say. He simply put his head down to rest on top of his crossed paws and closed his eyes in readiness for a nap. I shook my head, dismissing him, and stripped down to my bra and panties, all the time wondering if maybe I was the one losing my mind.

Scotty returned after a few minutes, holding a thick garment cover, which was carefully folded over his arm. He unzipped it, and I waited in anticipation despite my misgivings. I looked in awe when he removed from it the most beautiful skirt I had ever seen.

"It's a Gustav Beer," he announced, stars in his eyes.

From memory, Gustav Beer had been a German designer active in France during the early 1900s. The skirt Scotty held out for my inspection consisted of a floor length, bell-shaped garment made of the finest muslin with exquisite machine lace, tulle, and embroidery thread around the bottom. The fine material was pure white. I drew in my breath at its beauty.

"Oh, Scotty, this is divine! But I can't wear something like this; it'd be ruined. I'd get grass marks on it."

Scotty ignored me. "Try it on, along with this." He held out a pastel yellow peasant-style, silk top that looked more contemporary, but vintage, nonetheless.

I put on the garments and paraded in front of him. "This is so light. I feel as if I'm dressed in wisps of cloud," I remarked, loving the feel of wearing something so valuable.

"Enchanting," Scotty pronounced with a dreamy look on his gaze. "It could have been made for you, so consider it an early Christmas present," he stated.

I turned to the mirror and couldn't believe how small my waist looked. I was slim by nature, but the skirt with its flaring bell bottom and thick, tapered waistband, made my waist look like Scarlett O'Hara's in *Gone with the Wind*—an eighteen-inch waist—well, almost.

I fell instantly in love with the outfit. It was feminine, summery, and not one bit over the top. The peasant blouse gave it an almost ethereal look. "Oh, Scotty!" I remarked, my eyes full of gratitude. "Are you sure? This is so valuable."

"My dear," Scotty replied, regarding me with affection. "You've had a rough trot with Josh this year, so you deserve to pamper yourself."

"Thank you. Oh, thank you!" I was moved to tears. "I really appreciate it, and I'm glad you're my friend."

Scotty crossed over to me and planted a kiss on my cheek. "Always," he assured me.

It was an emotional moment for us. I was an orphan, and Scotty was alone in Sydney, too; his mother living in England and his father long dead.

"We are family," I uttered, and hugged him in order to hide my emotions.

Scotty held me close, and a meow of protest suddenly came from the bed. "You, too, Henry," Scotty added for the cat's benefit.

Henry looked satisfied and went back to sleep.

Sunday dawned sunny and clear with a mild breeze—a perfect spring day and just right for a picnic. Rick picked me up from Scotty's place at eleven in an elegant silver-grey BMW convertible, and when I saw him alight from the car to hold the passenger door open for me I was glad I'd taken the trouble to dress for the occasion.

Rick was wearing a pair of casual tailored pants in a bone colour with a dark green silk shirt, open at the neck. His hair was swept back from his face even though a stubborn lock kept falling over his eyes. I still couldn't believe how much like the actor he really looked. I was sure he was constantly taken for Hugh Jackman.

"You look wonderful," he declared and kissed my cheek.

I settled in my seat, fairly sure I was blushing, and feeling rather confused. "Thank you," I said, avoiding his eyes and looking for my sunglasses inside my bag. Rick put on his own sunglasses, and we were off. "So where are we going?" I hoped he hadn't planned taking me to the beach. The sand was sure to ruin my outfit.

"Centennial Park," he answered. "The closest I can get to Central Park in NYC."

"I never thought of that," I remarked. "I guess Centennial Park's pretty big, but not as big as Central Park. Still, Sydney's not as big as New York City. Do you miss it at all?"

"You mean New York?" Rick kept his eyes on the road ahead.

"Yes."

"Sometimes I do, but mostly I don't. I've lived here a long time now, and you could say I'm more of an Aussie than a Yank."

I laughed. "True. Even your accent's become really soft, and if I didn't know it, I would never have picked you for a New Yorker."

"Oh?" He glanced my way quickly.

"I would've thought you were an Irishman in transition to becoming an Aussie."

Rick laughed at that. "This from a woman who judging by her last name is Irish or am I wrong?"

"You're half right, actually. My dad was Irish, but like you, he lost his accent after living here for many years. Come to think of it, he sounded pretty much as you do." Perhaps, this was a subconscious reason for my being so attracted to Rick. After all, it was often said women gravitated to men who were like their father.

The journey from Paddington to Centennial Park was short, and within ten minutes we were driving through one of the huge, wrought-iron gates at the park and down a tree-lined driveway.

Rick drove slowly in case a cyclist or horse rider should cross our path, and after a few more minutes, he pulled up at a spot where weeping willows were hanging over a tranquil lake, mostly populated by wild ducks and seagulls.

I noticed we were the only humans around. "Wow," I exclaimed, getting out of the car before Rick had a chance to open the door for me. "Is this a secret spot of yours? Where are the other picnickers?"

"Probably in the more popular spots near the kiosk," he replied while getting a picnic basket and blanket out of the boot. "I discovered this place when I jogged past here one morning and thought it perfect for a private picnic."

My heart did a little somersault at the word "private", but I guessed he meant we wouldn't have kids running all over us playing ball or throwing a Frisbee.

We sat under one of the trees and Rick unpacked a hamper full of goodies—chilled white wine, cold chicken, a tub of cherry tomatoes, another of black olives, diced avocado salad and crusty French bread. He even brought chocolate mousse and fruit salad for dessert. I said goodbye to my illusion of an eighteen-inch waist and tucked in at his invitation.

While we ate, we talked about many things, especially antiques and the arts, but later as we relaxed over the wine, I became more daring and asked the question I had been dying to ask since I met him.

"You said you came here because of your wife. So how long were you married?"

"Almost thirteen years," he stated, not at all put off by the question. "Denise and I met in New York while she was working for the New York Times."

"She's a journalist?" I asked, and decided to google her later. I was curious as to what type of woman would attract someone like Rick.

He nodded. "Yes. But she gave it up after a few years, especially because she started to miss her family over here. So we made the decision to move to Sydney."

"And you sold your business in New York before you came out?" I remarked casually while watching a duck fly in for a smooth landing on the lake. I didn't want to seem too nosy.

Rick refilled my wine glass. "Yes. I thought I'd explore possibilities in Sydney. At first, I consulted to a couple of five-star establishments as Head Chef, just to get to know the restaurant scene. Later, when Denise and I split up, I was in the middle of getting Rick's Café established, and it was starting to go really well, so I stayed on."

Why did you split up? This was what I really wanted to ask, but I knew it wouldn't be polite. If he wanted me to know, he'd tell me. I also wondered whether there had been children from the marriage. After all, thirteen years was a long time to be married without kids, and perhaps this was one of the reasons Rick had remained in Australia. If so, this probably meant he still saw the mother of his children.

A wave of jealousy swept over me, and I told myself to stop being stupid. The man had asked me out on a date, and I was already jumping ahead to how I would cope if I had to meet Denise for the

70

sake of the kids. Thankfully, just at that moment, Rick changed the direction of our conversation and we went back to safe ground, conversing about antiques. I told him about a few pieces Scotty had put aside for his consideration.

It seemed like we had been there for a short time, but when I glanced at my watch, I saw it was close to four in the afternoon, and it was beginning to get rather cool. Rick suggested we go back to the café for coffee, but I told him I was too tired and would take a raincheck.

The truth was I could only take so much of Rick's magnetism without my hormones going haywire, and keeping them under control made me feel exhausted. Besides, I didn't want to come across as being too eager, plus I simply had to get back on the net to find more dates. My blog post was due in a few days and I was really scraping the bottom of the barrel.

Rick didn't insist when I declined his invitation. He was the perfect gentleman and after we packed up, he saw me safely seated in the car and drove me home. We pulled up outside Scotty's and I was grateful he was still at the shop. I didn't exactly relish the idea of his peeking out the window when he heard us pull up in case Rick wanted to kiss me. I knew I wanted him to kiss me, but I didn't want anybody watching.

"Well," I spoke as the car came to a full stop, "thank you for the wonderful picnic. I really enjoyed it."

"So did I," Rick stated, looking at me in a rather intimate way.

I swallowed hard—nervous as anything—and closed my eyes when I saw his face move toward mine. He brought his lips to touch my mouth in a soft, almost chaste, kiss. It was as though he was testing the waters. The waters are fine! I wanted to shout out. But he withdrew too soon, and I felt cheated.

His gaze was intent as he regarded me. "I really enjoyed your company, Cat, but I don't want to rush anything, not with your vulnerable state concerning Josh."

So that was it. He was being caring and sensitive about my feelings. He thought I was on the rebound from Josh, and in a way I was even though I'd made the decision to let go of the past.

At that moment, Rick Blake scored all the points on my Man Eligibility Scale and took with him the bonus points as well. I gave him a total score of twenty points—even though my eligibility scale only went up to ten—and I knew right then that I was ready to marry him.

CHAPTER 10

I was still staying with Scotty, namely because Mark hadn't called, but mainly because he hated being alone. I didn't mind—I lived in luxury, and saved money by not having to buy groceries. I insisted on paying for my share, but Scotty wouldn't hear of it. He argued that it was great to have me around because I took away many of the chores in the house and looked after Henry when he was travelling on business. So the whole thing worked out pretty well.

Once again, he tried to convince me to give up my place and move in with him, but the thought of Mark coming back into his life at any given moment held me back. I said to Scotty if by three months' time Mark did not return, I would move in.

Mark's things were still all over the house. Most of his clothes were in the wardrobe, his computer in the study, and his treadmill and weights in the guest room where I slept. Until Mark removed his things from the house, I wouldn't feel comfortable. Besides, Mark didn't like me. He knew I always advised Scotty to break it off. His main problem with me, however, stemmed from the fact I had known Scotty a lot longer than he, and Mark was jealous of the strong bond of friendship Scotty and I enjoyed—one that was difficult for him to break.

After Rick had dropped me off on Sunday, I changed into comfortable track pants and T-shirt, and lazed about Scotty's quiet terrace for a while, soaking up the last of the afternoon sun. This was followed by a nap with Henry curled up near my head. When I woke up, I jumped on the internet and checked my emails.

There was one from Peter, the serial killer, asking if I would like to have coffee with him again. Yes, in another life, I thought; but I replied nicely, thanking him for our last meeting. I told him for now I was pursuing another potential relationship and that I would rather focus on one person at a time. I mean, what could you say to someone you never wanted to lay eyes on again without insulting them? Hm. Good topic for my next blog post: How to get rid of the "no-gos".

I tried not to think too much about the blog, or the dating side of things, and definitely not about Rick and his kiss. I didn't want to build up my hopes as far as he was concerned. For all I knew, he had ten girlfriends tucked away, and he had gone out with me out of pity. He had, after all, given me a chaste kiss before sending me on my way with the excuse that I was still too vulnerable. I didn't understand why I was trying to find fault with him rather than believing he had been genuine. Stop thinking about Rick! I told myself as I turned back to my emails.

There were at least thirty or so "Let's meet" requests. I became so engrossed checking the profiles that I lost track of time and before I knew it, Scotty was home. He popped his head into my room.

"How was your date with Rick?" was the first thing he uttered.

"Can we talk about it later? I'm doing some work now," I replied in order to buy time. I didn't want to talk about Rick, not when I had to select someone to date out of the profiles I had been perusing.

Scotty glanced at his watch. "It's past seven and I'm starving. What do you say to Thai? We can go down the road to Frangipani."

"Okay," I agreed, "but give me a few minutes to finish this."

"I'll go and shower. I'm dusty after unpacking the new shipment. You've got twenty minutes," he stated and disappeared down the hall.

I turned back to the profiles and came across a pleasant-looking guy named David. In fact, on closer inspection, I had to admit he was rather cute with curly brown hair, green eyes, a nice smile, and an athletic-looking frame.

David was a home renovator/restorer and ran his own business. He lived locally and was thirty-five years of age. In his profile, he stated his dating age range as 30 to 45 years. Not bad. It seemed David was more open-minded than most of the guys I had seen on the site who were always looking to date someone at least ten years

74

their junior. I emailed David and suggested we meet at Rick's on Wednesday evening. Luckily, he happened to be online just as I sent the email and we chatted for a few minutes before agreeing to meet at six. Once I signed off, I went to get ready for dinner.

I wasn't sure how I was going to face Rick after our date on Sunday, but I was in luck. When I arrived for my meeting with David on Wednesday evening, Mohsen showed me to my usual alcove and got me a cappuccino without my having to ask.

I looked around nervously in case Rick should appear at any moment, but Mohsen was ahead of me, and as he set down the cappuccino on the table, he said, "The boss has a night off, Miss Ryan." Then, he went on his merry way, and I was left to wonder what that meant. Did Rick have another date? Every time I came here, he was working. So how come he now took the night off? Where was he?

"Cat?" I jumped from my chair and looked up to see David standing in the alcove with an attractive smile on his face. "I'm sorry I startled you. You must've been deep in thought."

Wow! He was cuter live than in his photo. He had a boyish look and a deep tan that accentuated his green eyes. "David, hi! Sorry about that, I was thinking about work," I explained and shook his hand.

David took a seat opposite me. "That's right, you work with antiques," he commented. "As you can imagine as a home renovator, I take an interest in that kind of thing, especially since a lot of my clients have homes they want restored to reflect their former glory."

I took an instant liking to him. He was charming, good looking, and unassuming. He was also laid back and a good conversationalist. In fact, I liked him so much that after we finished our drinks, I accepted his invitation to stay on for dinner.

"After all," he remarked, "we have to eat, and it's getting late. Besides, I want to talk some more about antiques."

This was the magic word, and I agreed readily, safe in the knowledge that Rick wasn't around.

"I'm thinking we might be able to do some business," David said after we ordered.

We'd decided to order a Moroccan platter for two, which was a combination of five dishes that patrons could try as an introduction to Moroccan cuisine. This sounded fun, and we went for it.

"A lot of my clients live in Bellevue Hill, Vaucluse, and here in Woollahra," David continued.

All expensive suburbs full of rich people, I thought. This might lead to good business for the shop.

"Anyway," David went on, "I don't really mix business with pleasure, but I thought I would drop by your shop, if that's okay, and see what kind of pieces you carry. I may be able to use some for the homes I restore."

"Yes, that would be great. I'll give you a business card before we leave—you'll want to talk to my boss in any case, I'm just the part-time help."

"And very charming help at that," he smiled, and suddenly I was glad I had met him. Though for some reason, I didn't feel quite the same sexual tension I'd felt when I was with Rick, and yet, I found David just as attractive. Don't go there, Cat, I said to myself. Just enjoy the evening.

We ended our meal with coffee and dessert and by talking about art and restoration. When I asked David for the time, he informed me it had just gone eleven.

"Wow! Talk about time flying when you're having fun," I exclaimed, "but it's time to go. I have work tomorrow."

David asked our waiter for the bill and refused my offer of money to pay for my half. "Please, Cat. I never let the woman pay, not even if things don't work out. Call me old-fashioned, but that's how I am."

Where have you been? I asked silently. And why hasn't some woman snatched you up by now?

David must've read my mind, and he threw me a boyish smile. "I've been on several dates, but not once did I feel any mental stimulation with the girls I dated. You're the first person I met through this site whom I'd like to see again."

Talk about smooth. "Oh." I just didn't know what to say to something like this. David was the perfect gentleman, and the perfect date. Rick had tough competition.

David paid, and we made our way to the door. Mohsen saw us off with a little bow and for a moment, I hoped he wouldn't go blabbing to Rick about having seen me with a client who stayed on for much longer than an hour.

At the door, David took hold of my hand and kissed it. "I really enjoyed meeting you, and if it's not too soon, I wonder whether you'd like to see me again."

Are you kidding me? But all I voiced was, "That would be nice, David. I enjoyed our time very much." I reached into my bag and drew out Scotty's card. "Here's that business card, by the way. You have my mobile number already or you can call me at the shop."

"I'll call you in the next couple of days and if you're not busy on Saturday night, perhaps we can go out for dinner again?"

"I'll check." I didn't want to sound too eager. "Give me a call and we can confirm."

We said goodnight and parted company, and I went straight home, falling asleep with a smile on my face as soon as my head touched the pillow.

Cat Ryan's Dating Blog #4

Well, it's true what they say—you have to kiss a lot of toads before you find the prince. But hey, don't get excited, ladies. I didn't find the prince just yet, but I think I'm getting closer to it.

I met a great guy and all I can say is that he surpassed all my expectations; but perhaps I'm rushing this. I've only been on one date with him—which was really our initial meeting. Still, we had dinner, and he paid. And get this: he says he always pays, even if the meeting doesn't go anywhere!

Ladies, there is a God out there after all and He's made a limited model of this kind of man, but at least He is giving us some hope.

Onto other things! How do you get rid of the "no-gos" without giving offence or making anyone feel uncomfortable? I suggest we choose prior to the initial meeting how we are going to do this. Better to be prepared. There are three options we should consider:

1. Face to face
2. Telephone
3. Email

If we're going to do it face to face—which is the most difficult way—we have to work out exactly what we're going to say. The most neutral excuse, and one which doesn't give offence, is that we feel we don't want to pursue the matter further.

This will suffice with most men, but be prepared for those who will challenge you and ask why you don't want to pursue it. Therefore, it's probably easier to do it via the telephone (preferably text message) or email. Try to keep it simple. Don't go saying he's too short or too fat or too needy. Simply say you feel you're not suited. Comments and suggestions are welcome.

I finished off the blog post by answering a whole bunch of Q&As on the "Who should pay for what" debate, which was still a hot topic, followed closely by "What if he's so repulsive I can't even stay for the duration of one cappuccino?"

David called a couple of days later and I agreed to go out with him on Saturday night. Not only this, but on the day before our date, he dropped by the shop and had a long talk with Scotty about several pieces that might be of interest to his clients.

After he left, Scotty joined me at the sales counter, where I was adding items to our inventory on the computer, and gave me a big smile.

"What's that for?" I asked.

"Darling, he's a gem!" Scotty declared. "I'm jealous. If he was gay, I'd go for him in an instant."

I smiled. This was the discussion we always had whenever we saw a cute guy. "Well, lucky for me he's not gay, then."

"But what about Rick?" Scotty remarked, watching my face for any sign of conflicting emotion.

I disappointed him by keeping the smile on my face. "What about him?" I said, smarting a little. "One chaste kiss and no call afterwards? I'm sure he knows I was at the café on Wednesday. I know Mohsen keeps him informed on every move I make, and he doesn't even call for a whole week?" I was disappointed I hadn't heard anything from Rick, but if this was the way he wanted to play it, then so be it.

"How do you know this Mohsen guy tells him everything?"

"I imagine he does. Why else would Rick tell him to give me my usual alcove whenever I come in? He's obviously keeping an eye on me. He practically told me so when I had the incident with that Peter guy, the creepy serial killer."

78

"Whatever," Scotty dismissed my assumptions about Mohsen reporting to his boss about me. "But it seems you're upset, Miss Ryan, and that's why you're sweet on this guy."

I glared at him with indignation. "No way! David's a nice guy, period. My agreeing to go out with him a second time has nothing to do with Rick Blake's failure to call me."

"Hm." Scotty threw me a look of disbelief. "I think you've got it bad for him. Come on, darling, admit it."

"You're wrong, Scotty. Sure, I find Rick attractive, but he's not really my type. He probably has girlfriends all over the place, and he hasn't given me a second thought since we went out anyway. If he had, he would've called."

Scotty still regarded me with disbelief.

"Okay!" I exclaimed. "I thought I was developing feelings for him, but I see I'm wasting my time. So can we drop it?"

"Very well," he replied. "Anyway, you know I'm teasing you. This David seems really nice, and after that bitch, Josh, you deserve a nice man in your life."

I laughed and gave him a hug. "I love it when you call Josh a bitch. Somehow, it makes him sound lower than pond scum."

"My dear, bitch or not, he was always pond scum as far as I'm concerned," Scotty returned just as I happened to glance toward the front entrance.

"And speaking of pond scum... " I left the rest of what I was going to say hang in the air because at that exact moment, the door opened and Mark walked in.

CHAPTER 11

That evening, I moved back to my place so Scotty and Mark could work things out without my being in the way. Scotty didn't want me to go, but I wasn't going to stick around and watch Mark talk him into forgiving him one more time.

It pained me that someone as nice and clever as Scotty could be so blind when it came to a cheating scoundrel like Mark. But as we all know, it's always easier to be wise when we're on the outside looking in. Scotty would simply have to make his own journey on this one, and hopefully realise Mark was not for him.

I could see why it was difficult for Scotty to let go. He and Mark had a lot in common—they loved travel, art, antiques, and all things luxurious. They lived the high life, and Scotty could certainly afford it with his thriving business and the smart investments he had made over the years. Mark was also well off, having inherited money from his father plus earning a very good salary as a senior flight attendant. In fact, he was a supervisor now, so the money was even better.

The two had met on a flight to Paris a couple of years back and shortly afterwards, Scotty had asked Mark to move in with him. Mark was sophisticated, witty, and very good looking. In fact, his physical looks reminded me very much of David's, the restorer I was dating, except Mark was in his early forties, though still a great specimen of a man.

Scotty liked older guys. Perhaps, it was a father figure thing because he lost his father while still quite young. And even though Mark was only twelve years his senior, he still pretty much

80

represented that sought-after father figure Scotty looked up to. It was the same with Scotty's respect for Rick Blake. He and Rick were good friends, Rick being around the same age as Mark. This probably had something to do with the reason Scotty was so keen for me and Rick to get together.

How did Rick find his way into my thoughts? Probably because I was depressed about being back in my spartan little studio apartment with no one to talk to. I looked around the one and only room with whitewashed walls and utilitarian grey carpet, a small kitchenette in one corner, a sofa bed and TV set in the other. The place had come fully furnished with a cheap Formica-topped table and four chairs, a scratched coffee table that had seen better days, and a sofa bed. The TV had been a housewarming present from Scotty.

Even though I disliked the place, I was lucky to pick it up at such a reasonable rate. After all, this was Paddington; and it was thanks to Scotty I had been able to secure the place. He knew the owner of the gallery, which was located below the studio. In the old days, the studio had served as a painter's workshop and the only good feature of the place was that it had an abundance of natural light, so all was not as gloomy as I saw it right now.

Despite this, I felt at a loss. Scotty was back with Mark, Rick seemed to have disappeared from the face of the earth, and I couldn't even ring a friend to talk about my feelings. The only women I knew in my age group were some old school friends. They were now long married with kids, and we had lost touch years ago. I occasionally kept in touch with some of the girls I used to work with at the magazine, but we were not close. Scotty still remained my closest friend.

I decided to get on the internet after I made a bowl of two-minute noodles. There was always someone online with whom I could chat. Then, I remembered I hadn't looked up Denise Blake, Rick's ex-wife, and curiosity got the better of me.

I didn't even know if she had kept her married name, but it was worth a shot, so I went into Google and typed in "Denise Blake + New York Times". I found about ten sites listing a Denise Blake, so I went to the first one. It was a story in the Wall Street Journal reporting the sale of Rick's Café for close to eight million dollars, and it mentioned the owners, Rick and Denise Blake, who had gone to live in Australia. The story went on to say Denise had been a

81

journalist with the *New York Times*, etc, etc. I looked up from the computer screen in thought. It seemed Rick and Denise had been co-owners in the business. I then scanned the rest of the story. No mention of kids anywhere, and no photos.

I quickly read through the other sites, but found nothing of interest except on the last one, where there was a small photo of Denise alongside a story she had written for the paper. The photo was in black and while and rather grainy. I could, however, make out a pretty face with long, dark hair, though the photo was outdated as it had been taken when Denise was still working in the States. I closed down the site and decided to check my emails instead.

There was no point in wasting time on any aspect of Rick's life. The fact he hadn't called still stung and was also an indication that the man had probably lost interest in me. So I was better off exploring my budding friendship with the attractive David and forget my feelings for the formidable Rick Blake.

Saturday arrived, and I spent half the morning trying to work out what to wear for my date with David. He was taking me to Tetsuya's and it was obvious he was a friend of the owner, seeing as the place was booked solid for a year, especially for Saturday dinner.

I telephoned Scotty at the shop. "What do I wear?" I always consulted him on matters such as this when it was a special occasion. He was the better dresser out of the two and knew a lot about women's fashion. I made a point not to ask about Mark.

"I'm helping a customer just now. Do you have time for coffee?" he asked, his tone giving the impression he was taking a business call.

"Scotty, you're busy. Don't worry about it," I remarked, not wanting to pull him away from his work.

"Darling," he exclaimed, "don't be silly. I'll get Mark to watch the shop for half an hour and we'll pop across the street to Lorenzo's."

"No, it's too much trouble. I only wanted your opinion over the phone, that's all."

"Where is he taking you?" Scotty asked.

"Tetsuya's," I announced, knowing what was coming.

Scotty drew in his breath and declared with trepidation, "Have you lost your mind, Cat? You're going to go to Tetsuya's and not consult with me on what to wear?"

82

I had to laugh when he put it like that. With Scotty, it was always an entire production. "This is the reason I rang," I pointed out.

"Be here by eleven. No arguments," he ordered and rang off.

I loved Scotty.

"Okay, let's go through the inventory," Scotty stated while we sat at Lorenzo's having cappuccinos and the house special— strawberry and ricotta cannoli pastries.

"I only have a choice of three outfits," I told him. "You know I'm on a tight budget. Fortunately, I got these when I was still freelancing for the magazine."

Scotty frowned. "What about your whole wardrobe? The beautiful clothes you owned when you were with Josh?"

I had forgotten about those. "I left them behind," I confessed.

"Why did you do that?" he asked in disbelief.

I knew he wasn't going to like my answer. "I didn't want to have anything to remind me of Josh, and most of the stuff I had, he bought for me. I used to attend a lot of his company functions and he wanted me to look nice."

Scotty scowled. "Well, you should've taken the whole lot with you. You deserve to have nice things."

I knew he was annoyed with me, but when I'd left Josh, I hadn't wanted anything at all reminding me of him, and this included the clothes he'd purchased for me. "Anyway," I stated in a light tone. "Let's not focus on the past. I still have some nice outfits."

"I'm sorry, darling." Scotty patted my hand. "Of course, you would look nice in a potato sack."

I was touched by his compliment. "How wonderful to have a supportive friend like you." I squeezed his fingers. "Now, let me tell you about the outfits, though you've probably seen them all."

He nodded. "Remind me, anyway."

"Okay, I have the little black dress by Alex Perry. Then, there's the Lisa Ho buff and mocha outfit; and lastly, the Donna Karan red dress."

There was approval in Scotty's eyes as he gazed at me. "Of course, you look gorgeous in red," he commented. "What about shoes?"

"Black patent leather Jimmy Choo's or Donna Karan strappy sandals, but they have a four-inch heel and they're not as comfortable as the Jimmy Choo's," I informed him as if he were my personal dresser. I felt like laughing, but Scotty took the whole thing seriously, so I remained composed and waited for his response.

"Well, the red would have to go with the strappy sandals. However, if you wear the black, you'd get away with the Jimmy Choo's."

The master had spoken, and I made my choice. "Black dress and Jimmy Choo's it is," I concurred.

Scotty nodded his approval. "Very well." We laughed. This was so much fun.

That evening, I met David outside Tetsuya's. He gave a low wolf whistle when he saw me approach, and I blushed. He looked very smart in tailored black pants and a black silk shirt with a casual, but elegant tan jacket. His boyish smile made him look much younger than he was. Next to him, I felt like a hundred, but judging from his reaction to my appearance, I was a sexy centenarian.

"You look wonderful," David remarked as he greeted me with a peck on the cheek.

"David," I said before we went inside, "this is a super expensive restaurant, and I don't feel right going in unless you let me pay for my half."

He frowned. "Hey, remember what I told you when we met? I'm an old-fashioned guy."

"I know, and you're very sweet, but I insist," I affirmed.

This was our second date—or first date seeing as the last one had only been an initial meeting. Therefore, I didn't feel comfortable with him paying, and I wouldn't have any fun unless he let me pay my way. We discussed this for several moments, but I wasn't going to budge, and in the end, I won.

"If I can't convince you otherwise, I guess I'll have to give in. I want you to know, however, I'm doing this under protest," he declared with a look of mock admonishment on his face.

"I feel better this way," I replied. "Thank you."

"Well, I've never been thanked by a lady for letting her pay her own way, but what the heck!" He smiled and ushered me inside.

We were shown to a private corner of the dining room overlooking a large courtyard with manicured Japanese gardens. The lighting inside was low and the atmosphere intimate. David ordered a Hunter Valley Semillon while we glanced through our menus to find out what was on offer.

84

Tetsuya's was a degustation menu, and I noted that among the delicious fare there was chestnut soup, pancetta-wrapped quail breast with sprouts, sashimi of kingfish with black bean and orange, fillet of barramundi with grilled artichoke, and a host of other scrumptious dishes.

During the meal, we talked more about antiques and restoration, and David regaled me with some funny stories about several of his clients and their taste in décor. We laughed a lot, and I felt more attracted to him by the minute. We finished off our meal with Nyoho strawberries sprinkled with candied pistachio and King Island cream. The food was superb, and the company wonderful. I sat back in my chair with satisfaction, knowing if David asked me out a third time, I would definitely let him pay.

Just then, my gaze landed on two diners across the room from us. One was Rick Blake, the other, a woman with long, dark hair. My heart skipped a beat, and I was saved from having to make explanations for my stunned countenance as the waiter arrived with our green tea. Thankfully, David did not notice the look on my face, and I recovered very quickly. Unfortunately, Rick did catch my look, and he excused himself from his companion and made his way across the floor toward our table. I did the best I could to paste a smile on my face as he approached.

"Cat," he stated in a rather cool voice, "fancy running into you here."

What a nerve, I thought angrily. How dared he come over to talk to me when all this time he hadn't even bothered to call.

I forced myself to smile again. "Hello, Rick," I greeted him, and then turned to David. "David, this is Rick Blake. He's the owner of Rick's Café." Then, I turned my gaze back to Rick. "Rick, this is David." I didn't bother to tell him what David did for a living in case he thought I was simply dining with a client. I wanted him to think David was my date—and, of course, he *was* my date.

The men shook hands. "Nice place you have," David addressed Rick. "I was there only last week."

"Yes, I know," replied Rick and then threw a look at me. "Mohsen told me you dined there."

Well, that was great! Now, he probably believed David was a client, albeit an important one if I was dining with him a second time.

"David knows Tetsuya," I announced, trying to salvage the

85

situation as best I could, "so he invited me to dine here."

Hopefully, he would get the message that I was on a date, but Rick didn't even bat an eyelid. He simply turned back to David and remarked, "That's great. I know Tetsuya, too. Great chef and excellent cuisine."

David nodded in agreement.

Suddenly, I wanted to hit them both, but before I could do anything crazy, Rick shook David's hand. "Well, don't let me keep you. Nice to meet you, David." Then, he turned to me, and his eyes held a mocking look. He knew what I had tried to do and it was obvious he didn't care. "Cat, I'll see you around sometime. You're looking very well, by the way." He turned and went the same way he came.

"He's a nice fellow," David remarked.

I nodded as I didn't trust myself to speak just yet. Then, I rummaged in my bag for my wallet, but David stopped me by holding up a hand.

"We'll settle up outside. Let me get the account with my credit card."

While David settled with the waiter, I threw a few glances in Rick's direction. *Who's the mysterious companion?* It looked very much like Denise Blake, but I couldn't be sure. Whoever it was, she was a stunning looking woman, and I couldn't wait to get out of the restaurant. I didn't want to be a witness to Rick's affectionate liaison with his ex-wife or one of his many girlfriends.

David offered me a lift when we went outside, and I accepted. I was sure I could trust the guy. Besides, Scotty knew I had gone out with him, and he had David's business card. If anything happened to me, the police would know where to look for my body. But I didn't think this was going to be necessary.

We chatted amicably all the way to Paddington until David stopped outside the gallery where I lived. "Well, thank you for a lovely evening." My hand went inside my bag to get my wallet.

David stopped me again. "Please, Cat," he entreated, "if you're so adamant about paying, I'll let you buy me dinner next time."

I smiled. Why not? "Very well. Thank you for dinner. It was lovely."

He reached across the seat and kissed me. I let him—all the time wishing Rick would drive by and see us. But what was I thinking? I was being kissed by a gorgeous man, and all I could do was wish Rick would see us.

It was then that the frightening realisation came to me—I was in love with Rick Blake.

CHAPTER 12

Cat Ryan's Dating Blog #5

What do you do if you meet two guys who are equally attractive, charming, and full of sex appeal? You fall madly in love with one of them, but he doesn't know you're alive; and you could potentially fall for the other one, but deep down inside you know you can't love him like you do the first guy. This is a bit of a moral dilemma. What are your thoughts, ladies?

This was my blog post for the week, and it was pathetic. I had nothing to say, but I was curious to know what the readers thought. It really was a true moral dilemma for me. I discovered I loved Rick, but he didn't seem all that interested. At the same time, I liked David a great deal, and had enjoyed his kiss, but I didn't think I could ever love him.

So what was I supposed to do? Give up on David simply because Rick wasn't interested or continue to see David and hope like hell I could forget about Rick? But this wouldn't be fair on David, of course. The thought kept going round and round in my mind, and I didn't know what to do.

In addition to this, I found myself in another quandary. The way I felt after discovering my love for Rick made me seriously consider ringing my editor to tell her I wanted out of this gig. I just didn't feel right writing the dating blog anymore. Besides, I couldn't see myself continuing to date guys under false pretences. I now had relationship problems of my own that I had to sort through.

After David dropped me off on Saturday night with his more than passionate kiss, I didn't wait for Thursday to post my blog. The fact that I raced straight to the internet only served to prove to me, yet again, that I wasn't in love with David. The minute he drove off, I went to the computer to post the one paragraph in desperation about my predicament. This time, I needed all the help I could get.

I slept badly that night, and in the morning I made a strong cup of coffee but didn't bother with breakfast. I immediately went online to check if I had any comments from my readers.

Dear Cat,

You don't see men being so noble and moral. I say keep your options open and keep dating the one you don't love. If you're lucky, the other one will get jealous and come after you. If he doesn't, then he's not worth two cents. Good luck!

Amy, New South Wales

Hi Cat,
Half your luck, girlfriend! I wish I was in your shoes.

Roberta, South Australia

Hey Cat,
If the one who doesn't know you're alive can't see you for the trees, take the other one and run.

Tricia, Queensland

Dear Cat,
Remember that once you turn off the lights, they're all the same. LOL.

Jo, New South Wales

Cat,
I wouldn't waste my time on the one who doesn't know you exist. Life's too short to throw it away on someone who's blind. Go for the other guy and make it happen. Remember, there are different kinds of love.

Bettina, New South Wales

Hey Cat,
At least your guys are attractive, so this is a good problem to have. As for

me, I've been kissing so many ugly toads I've lost count—and not even the barest hint of a prince yet.

Ally, Queensland

There were about forty or so comments, but Bettina's was the only one that jumped out at me. She was right—life *was* too short to throw it away on someone who was blind.

It looked like Rick was dating his ex-wife or someone who looked like her. After our picnic date, he hadn't made the slightest attempt to call me, and then he had the nerve to sound cool and superior when I saw him at Tetsuya's. What was his problem? It wasn't like he was interested in me. And yet, when he kissed me after the picnic, he said he didn't want to rush anything because I was still vulnerable as a result of my break up with Josh.

Could it be he was giving me time to get over my broken heart? This could explain why he was so cool when he saw me with David. Perhaps, he had known David was my date, and not a client after all, and he may have concluded that I couldn't possibly be nursing a broken heart if I was already dating someone else. Finally, there was the remote possibility that he may have been jealous, but somehow I didn't think Rick was the jealous type.

I finished my coffee and got ready for work. Scotty might have a better insight into this, and if I was going to analyse the whole thing to death, I may as well get his input.

Scotty was selling a pair of shabby chic bedside tables to a customer when I walked in at ten o'clock. After taking one look at my face, he excused himself and quickly walked over to me.

"Go and get us some cappuccinos from Lorenzo's, darling." He patted my shoulder. "I'll be through by the time you return."

I put my things down in the office and went across the road to get the coffees. I also decided to indulge in some Italian shortbread fingers, which were partially dipped in chocolate. Right now, I didn't care if they went straight to my waistline and hips. Coffee and chocolate were the only salvation for my mood.

When I came back with the goodies, we stood behind the sales counter, sipping our drinks and nibbling on the delightful shortbread fingers. "So what's going on?" asked Scotty.

"Rick was at Tetsuya's," I announced, my face grim.

"And what happened?"

"He came over to our table to say hello and was really cool toward me," I replied despondently. "I don't see where he gets off being like that when he was out with another woman!"

Scotty's eyes grew large. "Really? Who was she?"

"How should I know? But it looked very much like his ex-wife," I stated angrily.

"How do you know what his wife looks like?"

"I googled her," I confessed, "and she's his *ex-wife*."

Scotty's brows shot up. "Okay, but you're jumping to conclusions. You always do. This woman could very well be his ex, and maybe they had to catch up to talk about something or other; or she could simply be a business colleague. In fact, she could've been anyone, darling," he declared, trying to reason with me.

I pounced on him. "Do you know whether Rick's got kids? How long have you known him? Do you think he's trying to get back together with her?"

He held up a hand. "Hey, hold it right there." Then, he held up his hand again, this time in front of my face when I tried to speak. I sighed and stayed quiet. "Now," he spoke calmly, "let's take this step by step." And he started to count on the fingers of his hand. "One, I don't know if he's got kids—and if he has, he's never spoken of them to me. Two, Rick's been a client of mine for a couple of years. Three, I have no idea if he's trying to get back together with his ex. Besides, what's it to you?"

I took a sip of my coffee so I wouldn't have to answer.

Scotty threw me a knowing look. "Ah, I see. You're in love with him!" he declared excitedly.

I threw a quick glance around the shop to make sure we were still alone. "Keep your voice down!" Scotty was smiling like a Cheshire cat, and I wanted to slap him. "The truth is," I confided in a low voice, "I do have feelings for him, but he seems to have forgotten I exist."

"You're jumping to conclusions again," Scotty reminded me. "You don't really know why he didn't call in all this time, and you don't know who the woman is. So if I were you, I would stay cool and wait for his next move."

What Scotty said made sense, but I was cursed with an impatient nature and knew it was going to be murder for me to play it cool. "Hey, if he's been your client for two years, how come I've never seen him in the shop before?" The thought had just occurred to me.

"Rick's only been here a couple of times, and it was on days you weren't working. I normally deal with him over the phone. He tells me what he's looking for, and I scout around for it."

I drained the rest of my coffee and finished my shortbread fingers. Scotty eyed me with concern when he saw me glancing at one of his, which was as yet untouched.

"How did things go with David?"

"That's the ironic part," I replied with a feeling of frustration. "David's a really nice guy, and I find him attractive, but when he kissed me last night, I was wishing Rick would drive past so he could—"

"Stop!" Scotty interrupted. "Back up, back up. David kissed you?"

"Yes," I stated, as if there was nothing surprising about the fact.

"But this was your first date," he pointed out. "Officially, the first meeting doesn't count as a date."

"I know that!" I snapped at him. "And since when did you become such a prude anyway?" Honestly! I couldn't understand what had come over him.

"No need to bite my head off," he protested, trying to placate me. "I'm only asking. After all, you're standing here, telling me you're in love with Rick, and then you're off the next minute, kissing some other guy."

I raised my eyebrows in annoyance. "It wasn't like that," I uttered, and this time I spoke calmly. "David and I hit it off. He's a really cool guy, but it wasn't until he kissed me that I realised I was in love with Rick. I mean, here's this guy kissing me after our date, and all the time I'm wishing Rick would drive past and see us. That's when I knew I was in love with him."

Scotty gazed at me with a warning look. "Well, you'll just have to keep this to yourself."

I felt my temper rise and threw him an accusatory glance. "I'm only telling you this because you're my friend, and you were the one who wanted to know all the details."

"Never mind," Scotty's warning gaze became more insistent. Then, he smiled toward the door as he whispered to me. "Shut up!"

What the... And then I froze as I saw Rick Blake walk into the shop. I quickly cleared away the coffee cups and shortbread wrappers, one of which still contained Scotty's uneaten shortbread.

"What are you doing?" Scotty whispered.

"Go and serve him," I exclaimed in a low voice and disappeared into the back office.

I heard Scotty greeting Rick, and the two men exchanged pleasantries for a few moments before they got down to business.

"We're a little quiet at the café today, so I came down to have a look at those screens you have for me." Rick's voice carried over the shop and I heard him loud and clear.

"Oh yes," Scotty replied, "the musharabi screens. They'll be perfect for those dining alcoves."

I heard footsteps and knew Scotty was leading Rick to the area behind the silk screen where he kept the pieces for his regular clients. For a while I could only hear the murmur of voices and assumed the men were talking about the pieces and trying to come to an arrangement regarding price. I relaxed, and my eye landed on Scotty's shortbread. One bite, just one bite.

"Was that Cat I saw when I came in?" The clear sound of Rick's voice sent me into a bout of coughing as I swallowed the wrong way and choked on a crumb.

I heard Scotty reply, "That was her all right." Then, he called out to me. "Cat, got a minute?"

My coughing subsided a little and I knew I had no option but to go out there and face the enemy. "Hello," I greeted Rick coolly when I came out and looked at him from across the sales counter.

He gave me an amusing smile and from the corner of my eye, I saw Scotty madly gesturing and pointing to his own mouth. For a moment, I thought he had taken leave of his senses and was berating me for having had a bite of his shortbread, but from his wiping motions, I suddenly realised I had chocolate on my face.

I felt mortified and excused myself, running back into the office to check my face in the mirror. There a smear of chocolate across my upper lip, almost reaching my nose. Oh, God! I wiped it off with a tissue and reapplied lipstick. Then, I checked the rest of my face in case there were crumbs sticking to me, but I looked fine. When I went back out, the men had smiles on their faces and I felt like a fool, so I took refuge in sarcasm.

"How nice for you that I can provide some entertainment," I uttered, looking daggers at Rick.

"Oh, be fair, Cat," Scotty tried to appeal to my sense of humour. "It was all in fun."

I raised a cool eyebrow at him, and he shut up. Rick wasn't smiling anymore, either.

"I'm sorry, Cat," Rick said. "Honestly, we didn't mean to upset you. You just looked very cute with chocolate on your face."

I stared at him with indignation. "Cute? A baby with jam all over her face is cute, but I'm not a baby!"

"Fair enough," he stated with a serious look on his face. "I'm sorry."

I didn't acknowledge his comment and addressed Scotty instead. "Was there something you needed help with?"

Scotty shook his head.

"In that case, I'm going out back. I'm updating the inventory." Then, I turned to Rick with an icy look. "Nice to see you again, Rick." I walked off before he could reply.

I was making pasta for dinner that evening and thumping the cooking utensils this way and that, still fuming after the day's events. What a nerve Rick had talking to me as if everything was hunky-dory. First, he gave me a cool hello at Tetsuya's and then he was making fun of me and calling me cute. I just didn't understand the man. He was infuriating.

While the pasta cooked, I set a placemat on the coffee table together with fork, napkin, and a glass. I frowned—another dinner alone in front of the TV. Looking on the bright side, I told myself I'd had a wonderful dinner with David, and there was the promise of another date on the horizon even if I wasn't in love with him.

As if my thoughts carried across the air waves to him, my mobile rang and David's name appeared across the phone screen. "Hi there," he greeted me when I answered. "Just wondering how your day's been."

"Hi, David. I had a busy day." I told him about the items I sold and what fine pieces they were. I left out the bit about Rick and the chocolate-covered shortbreads, of course. "What about you, how are things?"

We talked for a few minutes about his latest project for a house in Bellevue Hill. "It's more like a mansion than a house," David remarked, "and this will keep me busy for the next few months." He went on to describe the house, its grounds, the views of the ocean, and how once he was finished restoring it, the value of the property would increase by several million dollars.

My pasta was cooked by this time and while I chatted with him, I strained it and served it with Napolitana sauce.

"Sounds like you're getting ready to eat," he noted. He had obviously heard my movements around the kitchen. "I won't keep you, but I wanted to ask whether you'd like to go for dinner on Friday night."

Why not? I thought. I decided I was going to take Bettina's advice. She had said there were different kinds of love, and I was going to give this thing with David a chance to grow. "I'd love to have dinner with you—but this time, I pay," I reminded him.

He laughed, and we made tentative plans before he rang off.

I was just about to sit down to eat when the doorbell rang. "And who could this be at such a time?" I called out loud, annoyed that my pasta was going to get cold. I went to the security intercom and talked into it. "Yes?" For a wild moment, I thought it might be Rick.

"It's me," Scotty uttered. "Let me in."

He sounded upset. I buzzed him up, and when I opened the door to let him in, I knew there was trouble in the air.

"Mark and I broke up for good. It's all over," Scotty announced as he walked in and plopped down on my sofa, his head in his hands.

I removed the pasta from the coffee table. "Let me get you some tea, and then we'll talk."

He nodded, and I went to make chamomile. "I interrupted your dinner," he stated with red eyes.

"Not a problem," I reassured him. "I'll reheat it later." I brought the teapot and two cups, and joined him on the sofa while he regaled me with the whole story.

"Mark's been seeing someone in addition to Eric in London. I saw them walking hand in hand in Surry Hills when I went to deliver a piece for a client this evening. Mark saw me, and when he got home, we had a huge row. So he packed his bags and left. Just like that." Scotty managed to take a few sips of the tea, and then his head was back in his hands.

I put my arm around his shoulders. "I'm sorry, Scotty, but maybe this is for the best," I tried to comfort him. "It's better you know once and for all. Mark was obviously not as serious as you were about the relationship. And you know once the trust is broken between two people you can never get it back. You gave him a chance already, and look where that got you."

Scotty nodded, still holding his head.

I sighed, feeling for him. "Why don't you let me take you home; and I'll stay over tonight. We'll make some dinner together."

"I couldn't eat a thing," he declared in a muffled voice, trying to fight back tears, "but I do want you to come over. In fact, I came here to ask you to move in with me."

"Oh, Scotty, that's lovely. But I don't want to be in the way, and if for some reason—" I started to voice my reservations about Mark's comings and goings, but he didn't let me finish.

"He's gone for good, Cat. He packed most of his stuff, and I'm sending the rest to him via courier in the morning. He moved in with his new lover." Scotty's voice broke, and he buried his face in his hands again while he sobbed.

I hugged him as a mother hugs a child, and he clung to me. This was my very best friend in the world, and I wasn't going to desert him. He had been there for me in my hour of need, and now it was my turn.

"It's okay. Don't cry anymore. I'm here for you, and we'll get through this together." I reached for some tissues and handed them to him.

He dried his face and gave me a watery smile. "Thank you. I really appreciate it."

"Hey," I remarked, ruffling his hair, "what are friends for? I'll move in with you, but I have to give notice to my landlord."

"Leave it with me." He sniffed away the last of his tears. "Rafe's a friend. He'll understand."

I smiled and kissed his cheek. "In that case, give me a few minutes to tidy up and we'll go—but only if you promise to eat something," I admonished lightly.

"Very well," he agreed, and this time he threw me a real smile.

96

CHAPTER 13

During the week that followed Mark's departure, Scotty settled down a lot quicker than I would have expected. I sometimes caught a certain look in his eyes, which told me he was grieving for his lost love, but on the whole, he seemed to be okay. He threw himself into his work, and the rest of the time he spent with me, helping with my move into the guest room that was now fully mine—no treadmill and no weights belonging to Mark.

In fact, Scotty had eradicated Mark's presence from the whole house; he even sold the ten thousand dollar papier mâché day desk, which he had purchased for him as a birthday present. I gathered from Scotty's tearful description of the painful departure, that Mark hadn't liked the piece enough to take it with him. *What a fool and how ungrateful.* Mark would get his one day. He would learn you couldn't go through life hurting others and not get hurt in return.

Henry was delighted to have me back, and this time for good. He spent his nights dividing his time between Scotty and me. He went to bed with his daddy, but at around three o'clock every morning, he made it his habit to use me as an aircraft carrier landing-pad. He ran into my room, jumped over the foot of the bed and landed on my tummy before settling down to sleep on top of me. The shock of having a ten-pound cat land on my body as I slept was enough to give anyone a heart attack. I soon remedied this, however, by sleeping on my side. So when he made his landing attempts, he now ended up beside me where he curled into me in spoon fashion or simply lay on my pillow around my head.

Scotty asked me to work the full week as soon as I was settled because he had a number of auctions he needed to attend. He informed me there would be heaps of pieces that needed to be priced and entered into the inventory database.

I didn't mind doing this as with each day that passed, I became more and more determined to quit my blogging gig. Scotty refused to charge me rent, and this lightened my financial load immediately. I insisted on paying for groceries and keeping house for him in exchange for rent, however, which was a mutually beneficial arrangement. For a gay guy, Scotty was a messy housekeeper, especially when it came to laundry and vacuuming. He could afford to have a cleaner, but he didn't want a stranger in a house filled with so many valuables.

One morning, after Scotty left for an auction, I rang the editor of the magazine to tell her about my decision regarding the blog. "The thing is, Lola," I said when I told her of my intention, "I really don't feel right dating guys as part of my research. Plus the blog is getting so many hits these days that comments made by the readers are virtually running it. In my opinion, all you need is a moderator to keep up with the correspondence. Besides, I don't want to take money from you now that I don't have so much to write about."

Lola was silent for a moment, and I could almost hear her brain ticking. She was a shrewd businesswoman and obviously trying to find a way to make this work for her and the magazine.

"Okay, Cat," she said finally, "I see where you're coming from. So how about you keep on it as the moderator and encourage guest posts by some of the ladies who write in. This will in turn generate more discussions, and you won't have to date anymore."

What a great idea; and all I had to do was ensure I replied to comments and every week invite a guest blogger. I didn't want to let Lola down, so this was a happy compromise for both of us.

"I'll do it," I declared, relieved I wouldn't have to date again, "but I won't accept payment from you. Not for this."

Lola laughed at the other end of the line. "You're a sweet girl, Cat, but I don't expect any favours. Keeping the blog running still takes time and dedication, so how about I pay you half the fee?"

"Done," I agreed, and we rang off. I still had a couple of dates to which I committed for the following week; but after this, I could stop dating. The other thing I decided was not to use Rick's Café any longer for meeting the last of my dates. Lorenzo's, which was just across the road from the shop, was a great Italian café and nice enough for meetings.

I was happy with this outcome and more than relieved that I wouldn't have to lay eyes on Rick Blake again unless he dropped by the shop when I happened to be working. By now, I was no longer holding my breath in the hope he would call.

The rest of the day was spent in a flurry of activity with dusting, tidying up the pieces in the shop, and helping customers. In the afternoon, I received a call from David to finalise our dinner plans. He suggested dinner at L'Incontro in North Sydney. I loved Italian food and accepted with alacrity, but not before reminding him that he had agreed to let me pay.

Scotty dropped in at the shop near closing time, full of excitement. "You'll never guess what I found today," he exclaimed, a big smile on his face.

It made me happy to see him animated so soon after his break up. Perhaps, he didn't yet miss Mark as much because he was used to his long absences due to Mark's job as a flight attendant.

"I have a feeling you're going to tell me," I remarked.

Scotty glanced at his watch, locked the front door, and flipped the Open sign over to Closed.

"Don't tell me the crown jewels were up for auction," I said in jest.

He laughed. "No, nothing like that. But I acquired a Louis XIV marquetry commode," he declared. "The real thing!" he practically squealed when he saw I wasn't jumping up and down with joy.

"How much was it?" was my immediate question.

"A hundred and fifty thousand," he said in a matter-of-fact tone.

My eyes widened. "You paid that much for what is just a chest of drawers?"

"Cat, what's the matter with you? This is a piece from the early 1700s. I have the full provenance on it. So who knows, this might have been in the Sun King's palace, and the king could have given it as a gift to the family who first owned it on the certificate I have right here!" he stated, waving the piece of paper in my face.

Scotty went on to show me a photo of the piece from the Sotheby's catalogue he had brought with him, and I had to agree the piece was exquisite. It was a marble-topped commode, gilt-mounted with red tortoiseshell, ebony, and horn marquetry. It certainly looked like the property of a king.

"It's breathtaking," I commented to an expectant Scotty. "Do you have a client for it?"

He threw me a sideways glance while still looking at the photo in the catalogue. "I was thinking of keeping it for the house," he replied casually.

Then it clicked. This was a gift to himself to make up for the break up with Mark. Some of us took comfort in food, alcohol, drugs or sex in order to help us with the pain of a broken heart. Scotty did it with antiques. It was a safer way to deal with grief, but certainly a more expensive one. Having said this, he was lucky he could afford it.

"Well, I love it," I announced and saw his eyes light up. I guessed it was very important for him to get my approval right now. "But how did Sotheby's find this in Australia? Normally, this kind of piece would be sold at a European auction."

"Yes, I know," Scotty replied, "but this came through the estate of a deceased French businessman who was quite rich and living in Sydney at the time of his passing."

"Well, congratulations." I threw him a smile. "It's definitely a great find."

Scotty smiled back, and my heart swelled with happiness for him. He was getting on with his life.

David and I had a wonderful dinner at L'Incontro on Friday evening. We were seated in the restaurant's courtyard, which consisted of an arbour-like structure surrounded by greenery and star jasmine interwoven in its timber lattice walls. The whole area was protected by a marquee-style roof, which kept out the cold. Inside, the atmosphere was one of intimacy even though noise levels were sometimes rather loud due to the number of patrons who filled the restaurant.

We decided to forgo dessert and moved straight to after-dinner espressos served with small almond biscotti. "That was great food," David stated. "Did you have enough to eat?"

I gave him a smile. "This is the face of a satisfied customer." I laughed. "I'm so full I can hardly move."

"Me, too. Care for a walk to help us digest all this?" he suggested.

I nodded, and once I settled the account, David drove us to the bottom of Blues Point Road where we parked the car and walked down to the Sydney Harbour waterfront. There was a small park here, overlooking the Harbour Bridge and Opera House on the other side of the shore, with the city skyline as a dramatic backdrop. The night was clear and the sky dotted with twinkling stars and a three-quarter yellow moon.

It was breezy by the water and I crossed my arms to keep warm. I had on the red Donna Karan dress but hadn't thought to bring a jacket. David saw this as the perfect excuse to drape his arm around my shoulders, and though this felt really nice, I wasn't quite comfortable with it.

During dinner, my thoughts kept wandering back to Rick, and I hadn't been fully attentive to my conversation with David. He didn't ask what was wrong, but I sensed he knew something was preoccupying my mind. I made every effort to keep my attention from wandering off again and succeeded in being attentive by the time we reached the coffee stage. Now, walking under the romantic light of the night sky with David's arm around me, I knew this wasn't going to work. I'd taken Bettina's advice to see if I could fall for a different kind of love, but it was no use. Much as I enjoyed David's company, it wasn't fair to him. I couldn't waste his time any longer.

"David." I turned to him. We stopped walking, and he removed his arm from my shoulders as faced me.

"Your mind's full of someone else, isn't it?" He hit the nail on the head.

I nodded. "I'm so sorry," I uttered, feeling terrible for what I was about to do. "I really like you, David. You're attractive and fun to be with, and a great conversationalist, but—"

"There's always a 'but'," he stated gently, putting one finger to my lips. "No need to explain, Cat. I think I sensed all was not right when I last kissed you. It was as if your mind was somewhere else, and now I can see it was."

"Thank you." I kissed his cheek. "Perhaps we should go."

"Yes," he agreed. We turned and walked back to the car in silence.

When David pulled up outside Scotty's house twenty minutes later, I turned to him. "I'm so sorry things didn't work out."

"Rick's a lucky guy. I hope he realises it," David said, much to my surprise.

101

"But how—" I began.

"It was obvious from the way you reacted to him at Tetsuya's," he replied.

"Was I that transparent?" I felt mortified.

"Hey, no need to worry about it. We can't help where our hearts lead us." He reached across the seat and kissed my cheek. "Good luck, Cat. It was great knowing you."

I felt horrible. He had been the perfect gentleman, and was gorgeous to boot. Why couldn't I fall in love with him?

"Maybe, I'll see you at the shop sometime." I didn't know what else to say.

"Maybe. Goodnight." His voice sounded rather subdued.

I gave him a sad smile and stepped out of the car. He drove off without waiting for me to go into the house and for a moment, I felt desolate. It was just after ten and the lights in the house were still on. As I turned to go in, the front door opened.

"I guess you're single again," remarked Scotty from the doorway.

When I saw him standing there, looking at me with understanding in his eyes, I lost my composure and ran into his arms. Scotty walked me inside the house and straight to the kitchen.

"Hot tea for you, darling, and a good weeping session," he ordered.

He needn't have bothered pointing out the weeping session bit because I was already crying. "What's the matter with me, Scotty?" I sniffed into the wad of tissues he placed in my hand.

Scotty put on the kettle and took out cups and saucers. "Nothing at all, except you've got it bad for Rick."

Like I needed him to point out the obvious. "So what do I do? Where do I go from here?"

Scotty sighed. "I wish I could tell you, Cat. I don't know why Rick isn't calling you, but short of asking him, there's nothing you can do."

I nodded in agreement and wrapped my hands around the teacup he placed in front of me. I felt cold all of a sudden and needed the comfort of its warmth. "It's frightening to love someone and know you'll never be with them."

"I know," Scotty replied, "but look on the bright side—we have each other for support." He smiled, but the smile didn't reach his eyes, and I knew he was still grieving for Mark. Scotty was trying to stay strong for me despite his own pain.

I sipped the hot tea and felt a little relief at what he had said. We were certainly lucky to have each other. Some people had to deal with heartbreak alone, without the support of a good friend. I couldn't imagine what that must be like.

CHAPTER 14

I had a meeting with Vincent, one of the two dates to which I'd committed before my decision to stop dating for the blog. We planned to meet at Lorenzo's for coffee, and even though it was a working day for me, I decided to take an afternoon break. It was easy enough to pop across the road from the shop and then go back to work after the meeting.

Lorenzo's was a small café housed in a quaint sandstone building that had been a house at some stage in its history. The place consisted of three smallish rooms; the main one at the front spilled out onto the sidewalk with its rustic timber tables and bentwood chairs. Vincent and I sat inside the front room as the afternoon sun was quite strong, and although the outside tables were protected by large sun umbrellas, the air was still and making it too muggy to enjoy the great outdoors.

"Looks like we're in for a hot summer," I remarked to Vincent.

He was a pleasant-looking man in his late thirties with brown hair and hazel eyes. He had a nice smile, and even though I didn't feel attracted to him, I thought we might become friends. I sensed he felt the same way about me, but I couldn't be absolutely sure.

This was the problem with internet dating. You only had a photo and profile to go by, and in the space of the time it took to have a coffee with the person, you had to make up your mind as to whether you were attracted to each other enough to make a second date. This placed a huge amount of pressure on people who met this way.

In a normal social situation, you had time to chitchat without the pressure of having to make a decision right there and then. Oftentimes, you had a chance to meet on several occasions, especially if you were part of a group sharing a common activity or hobby. Whatever the case may be, you had time to size each other up. With internet dating, it was tough. At least, I found it so.

A woman who worked in human resources had recently left an interesting comment on my blog. She said she often treated the "coffee meeting" like a job interview. By the end of the coffee, she pretty much made up her mind as to whether or not she wanted to see the guy again. She went on to say she often had up to three meetings a day on weekends, enabling her to get through six guys in the space of two days. I was fascinated by her account of how she rated the guys and the criteria she used to make a decision between the losers and those who made her shortlist.

After reading the account of how she organised and shortlisted her dates, I had to agree her method made sense. In a job interview, the interviewer had to decide in the space of a short meeting whether the candidate had the right qualifications and experience for the job, and whether there was a "fit" with company culture. Internet dating was essentially the same thing. Instead of qualifications and experience, however, you looked at personality traits and what the guy did for a living (this was very important because no woman I knew of wanted to be stuck with an unemployed man looking for a meal ticket). Finally, you decided if he fitted you and your lifestyle— plus you had to decide whether he had enough things in common with you in order to become a potential mate.

The waiter brought our coffees and I turned my focus back on Vincent. Time for the interview to start, I thought. "So, did you have trouble finding the place?" I asked—this was always a good icebreaker.

"Not at all," Vincent replied, stirring sugar into his coffee. "I used to work around here, so I'm familiar with the eastern suburbs."

Good opener, I thought. "What do you do?"

"I'm a chef," he answered. "I work in a big five-star hotel right now, but years ago I worked at Pruniers."

Pruniers was an upmarket restaurant in Woollahra, not far from Rick's Café. Stop it! I silently chastised myself. *Forget about Rick*. "That sounds great. Do you enjoy it?"

"I do," Vincent stated. "There are long hours and shift work, but

I love what I do."

Okay, so where to from here? "It seems being a chef is all the rage these days. Look at the likes of Jamie Oliver and Neil Perry; they're big celebrities now," I observed.

"Yes," he agreed. "I guess you could say that cooking is an art. So what do you do?"

"I work with antiques, but that's my bread and butter job. I'm actually a writer," I replied, thinking of my book manuscript, which was gathering dust. Lately, between the blog and working at Scotty's shop, I hadn't touched it. "I'm writing a book on Renaissance art," I added before he asked me the obligatory question every person always asks writers: *What is your book about?*

"Oh, that's wonderful!" he exclaimed. "I recently got back from a holiday in Italy, and Tuscany was my favourite place. All those frescoes, not to mention the treasures of the Uffizi gallery."

Okay, I thought, so we do have something in common. I must ask this human resources woman to be a guest blogger for me. Her formula was working quite well. We were now half way through our coffees, and I knew even though I wasn't attracted to Vincent, I definitely wouldn't discount him as a friend. I wondered how he felt.

"You know," Vincent remarked, "when I was over there, I picked up some excellent cooking tips, and I'm now working on a new menu for the hotel—modern Australian fused with Tuscan."

We talked for a while about different cuisines that could be fused together, and I remembered at Rick's Café they did Moroccan fused with modern Australian, and a touch of Asian. *Rick again. Stop it, Cat!*

"… the texture is a little hard on the palate," Vincent commented; and I realised I had missed the first half of the sentence.

What now? I nodded as if I was fascinated and gulped down the rest of my coffee.

"Oh, my God, that's Rick Blake!" Vincent suddenly exclaimed, and I looked up in alarm.

Sure enough, Rick had just walked into Lorenzo's and was ordering at the counter. I gazed down at my lap in the hope he wouldn't turn around and see me, but to my horror, Vincent waved his hand and called out to him. My stomach plummeted to my feet.

"Rick Blake!" Vincent greeted him. "How are you, mate?"

Rick turned. His eyes first landed on me. He didn't smile, but simply nodded a greeting. Then, as he turned to Vincent, his face lit up with a beam of pleasure. I bit my bottom lip and told my heart to stop beating like a drum. His smile sent desire coursing through my veins and played havoc with my hormones.

"That's an old friend of mine," Vincent informed me. "Do you mind if he joins us for a few minutes? I haven't seen him in years."

What else could I do but agree? Besides, I wanted to know how Vincent knew Rick.

"Got a couple of minutes to join us?" Vincent asked Rick, who was already walking toward our table.

"Vince," Rick shook hands with the man, "it's been ages. I thought you were going to drop by the café for a catch-up."

"I know, but I never got around to it. Too many long hours at work," Vincent explained, and then turned to me. "Cat, this is Rick—"

"Cat and I already know each other," Rick interjected and took a seat at our table. "I can only stay a minute as I only popped across the road to get a couple of cappuccinos." Then, he turned to me. "I came by to pick up the musharabi screens."

I nodded, but before I could respond, Vincent took over.

"Mate, how's the business?"

"Extremely busy," replied Rick. "It keeps me occupied most of the time."

"And how's Denise? I haven't seen her in ages." When Vincent mentioned Denise's name, my ears pricked up.

"Doing fine," Rick answered, and to my annoyance, he changed the subject. "What a surprise seeing you here, Vince. Is Cat scouting for you?"

For a moment, I didn't know what he was talking about, and then the penny dropped. Rick thought Vincent was one of my clients. *Oh, no!* And there was nothing I could do now. It was all going to come out in the open. Vincent looked puzzled, and Rick added, "I didn't know you were a collector."

Vincent laughed, and I felt my cheeks burn. "You mean antiques? No, no. Cat and I met through an online dating site. This is our first meeting."

I glanced in Rick's direction from under my eyelashes. He didn't seem at all fazed. "Well, in that case, don't let me interrupt you." He stood and held out a hand to Vincent. "Give me a call sometime, and let's have a drink at the café."

The men shook hands. "Will do," Vincent nodded.

Rick gave me the merest of nods but addressed Vincent. "My coffees are ready. Catch you later."

Vincent turned to me. "Talk about a small world. I used to work with him at Pruniers before he opened his own business," he explained.

"Oh." I tried to look interested, but I was too busy analysing Rick's reaction to his finding out I was internet dating. How long before he figured out that all the other so-called clients with whom I met at his café were, in actual fact, dates?

That evening over dinner at Frangipani, the Thai restaurant we frequented from time to time, I shared my concern with Scotty.

"Well," Scotty remarked, taking a sip of wine, "I don't see why you're getting all worked up about it."

I sighed with exasperation. "The man's going to think I'm a liar!"

Scotty gazed at me for a few moments before he stated, "But you are, my dear Cat, you are."

I rolled my eyes. "Thank you. That's really reassuring," I retorted.

Scotty laughed. "Hey, I'm just teasing. So you lied. Big deal. Besides, he doesn't know for sure whether some of the men you saw were clients or dates, does he? I mean, he'd only be assuming this, and he's got no proof beyond what this Vincent guy said."

Scotty made sense and I started to feel better. I helped myself to another portion of Massaman beef curry and pondered some more on the whole situation. At the end of the day, Rick hadn't exactly been forthcoming about Denise or why he hadn't called me, plus it wasn't like we were in a relationship. So what I did with my time was really none of his business.

"True. He has no proof," I agreed, looking thoughtful.

"That's the spirit," he replied with a smile, "and that brings me to a little request I have."

"Don't tell me you want to invite Rick over for dinner." I was joking, of course.

"Not exactly," Scotty responded, and I felt the hair at the back of my neck stand on end. Somehow, I knew his request was going to involve the object of my affection—and vexation.

"What's going on?" I threw him a suspicious look.

Scotty grinned. "Nothing that deserves the look you're giving me."

"Sorry," I smiled. "I guess I'm a bit on edge right now. What can I do to help?"

"I have two estate sales on tomorrow, so I need you to deliver something to Rick."

"But he was at your shop only today!" I protested. "Why didn't he take with him whatever it is you want me to deliver?" The thought of having to go to Rick's again and face him brought back all the concern I had about this afternoon.

"You don't understand." Scotty explained, "Rick ordered a couple of chandeliers, and they're being delivered to the shop tomorrow morning. I need you to clean them and enter them into the inventory before you deliver them."

"Well, can't it wait until you return?" I asked with dwindling hope.

"Unfortunately, no," Scotty informed me. "The estate sales are out Cessnock way and I won't be back till late in the night."

"Okay, so he can wait another day, can't he?" I just didn't see what was so urgent about the chandeliers that I had to drop everything and deliver them.

"Rick's catering for a wedding function tomorrow evening, and the chandeliers make up part of the décor. The wedding party is of North African-Arab extraction and they want to recreate a Moroccan feel."

"But the whole of Rick's looks Moroccan, so what's the problem?" I protested yet again.

"The function's taking place in a marquee tent at the family home and Rick is providing the catering off-site," Scotty responded, looking at me with concern. "Cat, it's no big deal, honestly. Rick may not even be there by the time you arrive at the café, so you can leave the package with his maître d'. I would send a courier except these are delicate pieces and I don't want them handled by anyone else."

He had a point. The one good thing was Rick would probably be at the site, as Scotty suggested, and all I had to do was deliver the chandeliers to his staff. Mohsen would more than likely be waiting for them so he could personally take the pieces across to the function. "Okay, I'll do it," I said, but I still had my reservations about this.

"Thank you." Scotty sighed with relief while giving me a look of encouragement. "I'm glad I can count on you, and don't worry; things always seem worse than we think."

Since when had he become so philosophical? Only a week before he had been moping around the house because of Mark, although in the last few days, he hadn't mentioned him at all. It was as if Mark had never existed. I wondered whether Scotty had discovered a secret formula for getting over a broken heart. If he did, I would invite him to write for the blog.

Speaking of blogs, when we returned home from dinner, I went online to check what was going on with mine. Lola told me I could pretty much start the guest blogging straight away, and I created a forum where internet daters could chat about their experiences. There were already a few active threads, and I was relieved. The blog seemed to be taking care of itself, so all I had to do was comment as the moderator and ensure the content posted was interesting enough to generate discussion.

There was one entry from a woman in country New South Wales that caught my attention. It was entitled: "Just because you 'click' doesn't mean happiness is around the corner."

I met a guy I was pretty much attracted to right from the start. He had his own business, was a great dresser, and had a cute smile. He was well mannered, charming, and a great looker, too. He paid for our coffees (always a good sign), and we even went on to have dinner. Ours was the kind of meeting where you just "click" and you can't stop talking for hours. You feel this great connection and you think here, at last, is a man with whom you can have a relationship.

At the end of the evening, he kissed me goodnight, and I spent the whole night thinking how lucky I was to have met him. After dating so many toads, I finally saw light at the end of the tunnel—but I was wrong. He never called back.

I wondered what happened. You know, you always ask yourself if you did or said something wrong. Maybe, there was a piece of food stuck between my teeth when he said goodnight and I smiled at him—that sort of thing. After I tortured myself for weeks on end, I pretty much gave up. I thought he must've met someone else after me or he simply changed his mind. Then, I remembered him telling me the name of his business. He was a photographer and ran a studio. I was curious to see if I could find out some clue about him, so I googled him.

110

It turned out his was a family business located a couple of towns away from the one where I live. He ran the business with his wife, and when I clicked the "About Us" tag on his website there was a photo of him with his arm around a pretty blonde lady holding a toddler in her arms. The caption under the photo read: "We are a family-run business and we treat our clients with integrity and respect." Then, there was a blurb about this guy and how he was happily married with one child and another on the way.

This goes to prove that even when you think you've found someone special, he may not be available. So now I'm going back to date more toads. I'm sharing this story because I want you to know that just because you "click" it doesn't mean happiness is around the corner.

Sadly Disillusioned, New South Wales

What a story! A two-timer—and just a couple of towns away from where he lived with his young family. Talk about taking risks. I figured the guy might have been a newbie at internet dating because he'd actually given the actual name of his business to Sadly Disillusioned.

I had to wonder what the motivation was with guys like these. Did they get cheap thrills out of just one date and a kiss or did they go hunting for someone they didn't particularly respect very much and try to go for sleazy sex?

Perhaps, Sadly Disillusioned had been lucky after all. It seemed the guy had genuinely clicked with her, and therefore he might have changed his mind about a sleazy affair. Instead, he probably moved on to someone he didn't respect quite so much. There were plenty of guys like this out there, and it suddenly hit me that the similarity of this woman's case with mine was too close for comfort.

This could explain the reason why Rick had never called me after our picnic date. Just like Sadly Disillusioned, I failed to work out what had happened between us. I thought we clicked, and I believed we had the promise of a relationship. I definitely thought he would call me again and ask me out on another date. But then, nothing; until I saw him at Tetsuya's with another woman. Could it be he respected me enough not to try to have a one-night stand, and therefore he moved on to someone else?

Yet, when Vincent and I bumped into him at Lorenzo's, and

Vincent asked about Denise, Rick hadn't even bothered to mention they were divorced, which convinced me the woman at Tetsuya's had indeed been his ex-wife or wife, if they were not yet formally divorced. So Rick could be like Sadly Disillusioned's man, he could be looking for thrills on the side, but still have a wife he's not prepared to part with.

On the other hand, it was possible I was being unfair to him, and I had the story all wrong. He did say at the end of our date that he thought I was still vulnerable in relation to Josh. So it could very well be he was giving me more time to get over my heartbreak. Then, when he discovered I was dating through the net, he probably felt he read me wrong.

Somehow, I couldn't imagine Rick being a sleaze, and yet I had seen him with another woman shortly after he dated me. I sighed, confused about the whole thing and still feeling the sting of Rick's rejection. Could it be I misplaced my love and was barking up the wrong tree with him? If so, it wouldn't be the first time. I did it with Josh, too. Feeling despondent, I turned to the computer and typed a reply to Sadly Disillusioned.

Dear Sadly Disillusioned,

I can relate to everything you say and would like to tell you, like thousands of other women, I've been there, done that. It's sad when women automatically think they did something wrong when a guy doesn't call them back. I would like to suggest there's something wrong with the guy if he cannot recognise the gem of a woman he has in front of him—and I mean you and all the women out there who have been through the same experience. I think we have a lot to offer, and if a guy can't see this, then the fault is with him and not us. Unfortunately, in your case, the guy was married, but for his own reasons, he didn't pursue you. Therefore, it's good to remember you got away relatively unscathed with this one. Good luck with all the other toads, and I hope you will soon find your prince.

When I checked the blog thread in the morning, there were over five hundred replies to Sadly Disillusioned's story, and I experienced a wonderful sense of comradeship while I read some of the comments. The women who replied were full of support and encouragement, and I was proud to be a part of the sisterhood.

I briefly wondered what my fellow sisters would say about Rick.

With this thought in my mind, I went to get ready for work. In the process, I psyched myself up for the possible meeting with him this evening when I delivered the chandeliers.

CHAPTER 15

It was surprisingly busy at the shop and the day flew by. I spent a few hours between serving customers cleaning the Moroccan chandeliers with a small brush. Despite this, it was difficult to get all the dust and spider webs from the delicate brass openings that had been cut by hand to create an intricate pattern. Scotty certainly had a special talent for finding treasures and exquisite antiques. These particular chandeliers were expensive reproductions, but beautiful all the same.

When the working day drew to a close, I took my time wrapping the pieces in readiness for delivery while I prayed Rick would be at the function, as Scotty had suggested, and not at the café. By five-thirty I could no longer delay and, after loading the chandeliers in the back of my hatchback, I set off. I hoped for red lights all the way to Woollahra, but as luck would have it, I only got green ones. It annoyed me as I thought that if you wanted to get somewhere fast you always got stuck with red lights, and when you wanted to delay, all you got was green. Perhaps, this was destiny's way of playing tricks on us mere mortals.

Upon arrival, I parked around the back of the building and walked to the front entrance, leaving the pieces in the car. My intention was to seek out Mohsen and get him to take delivery of the chandeliers. I certainly had no wish to run into Rick.

Luck was on my side for once, and when I walked in I met with Mohsen, who was standing at the maître d' station. "Good evening, Miss Ryan," he greeted me with a little bow. "Would you like your usual table?"

I smiled at him. "Not tonight, Mohsen," I replied, casting a furtive look around the main dining area in case Rick should be about. "I'm here to deliver a couple of chandeliers for Mr Blake's function. So if you would come with me to the car, I—"

"Oh," he interrupted me. "Excuse me, Miss Ryan, but Mr Blake will want to deal with this himself. Please come with me."

I struggled to find a reason for Mohsen not to take me to Rick, but he was already motioning for me to follow, and I had no option but to do so.

He started to walk in the direction of the kitchen. "If you will wait in Mr Blake's office, I'll only be a moment. And if you give me the keys to your car, I'll fetch the items."

The café was relatively empty; it was still early for the dinner crowd, and as we walked through the main dining room, I looked around quickly one more time, wondering where Rick was hiding. Perhaps, he was waiting for me in his office, but as I happened to glance up into one of the dining alcoves, I saw him sitting at a table with the dark-haired woman from Tetsuya's. They were having coffee and chatting in what looked like an intimate manner.

Rick caught my eye just as I was turning away, and I saw him stand. I hurried to catch up to Mohsen, who was almost at the kitchen entrance. "Mohsen," I called to him, "there's really no need to bother Mr Blake. I can see he has a guest. So if you'll just come to the car with me, I'll give you the chandeliers to take to his office."

Mohsen would have none of it. "Sorry, Miss Ryan, but I know Mr Blake likes to deal with this sort of thing himself." He glanced back toward the direction we had come. "In fact, here he comes now."

Mohsen waited for Rick to join us, and I shifted my weight from one foot to the other as I watched him cross the floor.

"Cat," Rick greeted me, "thank you for making the delivery. Scotty called and told me you'd be coming by this evening. Please step into my office." He led the way through to the back of the kitchen and down a narrow corridor where there was a dark green door with a brass handle. "If you'll give your car keys to Mohsen, he'll fetch the chandeliers."

I handed the keys to Mohsen and walked through the doorway as Rick held his office door open for me. When he closed the door

115

behind me, I turned and almost bumped into him, hesitating for a moment before moving a couple of steps back. His aftershave was doing things to me I didn't care to focus on right now.

"Honestly, there's no need for any of this," I protested. "I could've gone with Mohsen to the car."

"On the contrary," Rick showed me to a padded visitor's armchair by a dark oak desk. I sat down so my legs would have time to recover from the jelly-like feeling induced by the woody aroma of his aftershave. "May I offer you something to drink?" he asked as he walked around the desk and took a seat opposite me.

"Shouldn't you attend to your guest?" I pointed out, and instantly regretted it. The last thing I wanted was for him to think it mattered to me he had a woman waiting. Rick seemed not to have heard me or he was simply ignoring what I'd said.

Instead, he asked, "What can I get for you?"

I sighed in resignation. "A cappuccino, thanks." I didn't know what his game was, but it looked like I was going to have to play it.

Rick rang the bar for a cappuccino and ordered himself a macchiato. Then, he put down the telephone receiver and regarded me with an admiring look in his eyes. I squirmed slightly in my seat and hoped Mohsen would hurry with the chandeliers. "You're looking very well. So how have you been?"

I've been better, I wanted to say. "Busy, working. Scotty's out of Sydney and I've been at the shop since this morning, so it's been a long day." I directed my gaze around the elegantly furnished office and admired certain antique pieces that had come from the shop.

The walls were painted in a muted green and they complemented the polished timber flooring. On one wall was a large floor-to-ceiling dark oak bookcase, filled mostly with cookery books and hundreds of publications on food and wine. Behind me was a low matching credenza, covered with samples of different crockery and glassware as well as a vast array of lovely ceramic tagines.

"They're beautiful," I remarked, nodding toward the tagines. "Where did you get them?"

"I purchase them direct from Morocco. I have a local agent who looks after this kind of thing. We get a lot of our equipment from over there to maintain an authentic feel to the place."

"Oh." I nodded, and was vastly relieved when there was a knock on the door and a waiter entered with our coffees.

116

"Did Scotty give you the invoice?" Rick asked when the waiter left, closing the door behind him.

Good, we were talking business now. "Yes," I answered and fished around in my handbag. In my eagerness to avoid Rick, I'd forgotten about the invoice Scotty told me to pass onto him.

Rick took the piece of paper, accidentally brushing my fingers as he did so and sending a wild current of desire through my entire body. While he studied the invoice, I drank my cappuccino as quickly as I could with the intent of getting out of there immediately.

"I'll do an electronic transfer into Scotty's bank account and print out the receipt so you can take it back with you."

"Fine," I said quickly and kept drinking the hot coffee. I watched him furtively while he completed the transaction on his laptop and printed a receipt. There was a knock on the door, and Mohsen walked in and handed me the keys. I took them gratefully and swallowed down the rest of my drink. In a few moments, I would be able to make my escape.

"Boss, I put the chandeliers in your car," Mohsen informed Rick.

"Thank you, Mohsen. I'll be leaving in a few minutes, so please make sure you let Chef know."

Mohsen nodded and did his little bow. "Yes, Boss." He then turned to me. "Have a good evening, Miss Ryan." He left the room and closed the door after him.

I finished my coffee and stood. "Mohsen's a nice fellow," I remarked. "Is he also the real thing?"

"Yes, I sponsored him when he wanted to come here from Morocco," Rick answered. "He's been with me for almost the entire time I've had this business."

"Well, he certainly looks like a very loyal employee." I picked up my bag and held out my hand to him. "Thank you for the coffee, but I have to go now."

Rick came around the desk and shook my hand, and as I gently tried to pull away, he gripped it more firmly and my body was suddenly against his. His mouth came down hard on mine as his arms embraced me.

His kiss was passionate, and my body molded itself to his without effort as I surrendered my mouth with wild abandon. He had no problem invading it, and his tongue played with mine in an erotic

117

dance of desire. My arms wrapped themselves around his neck and I pressed myself closer to him.

"God," Rick whispered hoarsely when he came up for air and nuzzled my neck, sending shivers of delight all through my body. "I've been dying to do this for a long time, but didn't want to rush you into it."

I couldn't reply—I was putty in his arms, and putty didn't talk. Rick nibbled at my earlobe and his tongue circled the shell-like shape of my ear. "I went crazy when Vincent told me he was dating you," he confessed. "Right there and then, I knew I had to have you."

His words sent currents of excitement through me, but something nagged at me even though I couldn't think what it was. At that moment, I was incoherent, and all I wanted was for him to throw me across his desk and make love to me.

"Then have me," a voice replied softly, and I was shocked when I realised it was my own.

I heard a sharp intake of breath, and Rick was kissing me all over again—this time, with such fervour that I knew he could have his way with me and I wouldn't put up any resistance. I was half sitting, half lying across his desk, and he invaded me with his mouth, sending a hot surge of desire to the pit of my stomach, which travelled down to my pelvis.

Somewhere at the back of my mind, I hoped no one would walk in on us. Then, in a flash of insight, I knew what was nagging at me. I went cold all over and pushed Rick away from me as I sat upright. Rick's eyes were clouded with passion, and there was a puzzled look on his face. I stood, pulling down my shirt, which had somehow come up to my midriff; and though I still wanted nothing more than to have Rick take my body, I felt anger come to the surface, and with it came clarity.

"How dare you touch me! Might I remind you that you have a lady friend waiting for you out there while you're in here pawing me?"

A look of comprehension crossed his face. "You mean Denise?"

So it was Denise! My anger mounted. "Yes, that's who I mean," I spat out. "I don't know what game you're playing, Rick, but I'm not part of your harem." I made to walk out of the office, but he grabbed my wrist and pulled me to a stop.

"You don't understand," he declared, seemingly surprised, but

118

also upset. "Denise is—"

I pulled my arm from his grip and clutched my bag against me as if it would somehow protect me from him. "I know who Denise is, and if you think I'm going to get involved with a man who can't make up his mind whether he's married or divorced; then, you've got another think coming, mister!"

Rick looked astonished, and I could tell he was getting angry at the same time. "You don't know what you're talking about!"

"Oh, don't I?" I threw back at him. "Well, frankly, I think I do. And for your information, I don't play the role of mistress. So kindly get out of my way. I want to leave."

He looked at me for what seemed to be a long time, but in fact was only a couple of seconds. "I was never blocking your way," his voice was now gentle. "You're free to leave at any time."

I didn't wait for a second invitation and still clutching my bag to my chest, I walked out with my head up and my dignity in shreds.

CHAPTER 16

I never heard back from Vincent so I assumed he wasn't interested in being friends. After the chance meeting with Rick at Lorenzo's, we finished our coffees and parted without either of us voicing our intentions. Vincent mentioned something along the lines of seeing me online, and that had been that.

The other date to which I had committed was with a guy named Steve. We also met at Lorenzo's for coffee, and I knew straight away this was going to be a very short meeting. Steve was an accountant who had just come off a rather nasty marriage break up, and in my opinion he should never have started dating.

"Women say all men are bastards, but what they don't realise is that most men think women are real bitches." This was his opening line after we greeted one another.

What a charmer. I smiled at him over my coffee. "It sounds to me like you're dating too early," I suggested politely even though I felt like pouring my hot drink over his head.

Steve threw me a look of incredulity. "And miss out on the opportunity to meet someone nice? Just because that witch of an ex decided to make my life on earth a living hell doesn't mean I'm going to take it lying down. I'm going to get out there and meet other women."

It took quite an effort for me to control the sudden desire to lash out and tell him where he and his ilk could go, but I maintained my façade of civility. "I thought you said men thought all women were bitches. So now you're saying you're looking to meet someone

120

nice. Well, I guess that's a positive," I observed as if I was really interested in his opinion.

"You see," Steve replied, looking a little sheepish, "I was kind of generalising. After all, I think you're rather nice." His eyes went straight to my boobs when he said this, and I felt like gagging.

Dear God, this sleazebag was coming on to me straight after voicing his ugly opinion about women, and now he thought he could smooth things over. "It's good to know you think so, Steve," I declared and finished the last of my coffee in one gulp. I decided to drop my demeanour of politeness. "But I don't see myself with a man who thinks women are bitches, and irrespective of what you might say, not all women think men are bastards." I stood up and saw the look of astonishment in his eyes. "I'll pay for my own coffee on the way out," I informed him. "Good luck with your future dates."

I left him sitting there, mouth agape, and went back to the shop after I paid for my coffee. Thank God this was the last of my dates. If I ever decided to give internet dating a real go, it would be for a legitimate reason—like desperation.

I shook the depressing thought out of my mind as I entered the cool interior of the shop and saw Scotty serving a customer. He looked very excited about something. I could tell by the big smile on his face.

I hadn't seen him since his return from the estate sale he had attended as he had arrived home when I was already in bed, trying to sleep after the onslaught from Rick, which kept me awake half the night in any case. Then, by the time I was up the following morning, Scotty had already gone to the shop. I was only working a half day that day so I'd gone straight from the house to Lorenzo's to meet with Steve, and now I was ready to start my shift.

Scotty finished with the customer just as I put away my bag in the back office and made coffee—I needed another one after my meeting with weirdo Steve. When I came out holding two cups, Scotty took them from me, placed them on the sales counter, and put his hands on my upper arms as he turned me to him.

"Darling," he declared, his eyes bright with news he was obviously dying to impart, "you'll need to sit down for this one." He let go of my arms and gently pushed a stool toward me, which was behind the counter. "Sit, sit," he urged.

I sat down, taking in the bright eyes, the smile with the white teeth and the palpable energy of wonder emanating from him. I became caught up in his excitement even though I didn't know why. Perhaps, he's won the lottery, I thought. He certainly had that look about him.

"Okay," I said, "I'm sitting down. So what's going on?"

"Darling," Scotty said again, this time standing two steps away from me. "I'm in love!" His whole face lit up with happiness and he leaned toward me and gave me a big hug. I was still reeling from the surprise when he pulled back and searched my eyes. "Well, aren't you happy for me?"

"Of course I am, Scotty," I answered, "but you need to give me a moment to digest this." With a tinge of concern in my voice, I added, "I mean, you only recently broke up with Mark, and you suddenly spring this news on me. I must say it was the last thing I expected to hear."

Scotty's smile disappeared, and my heart went out to him. I got up from my seat and hugged him. "But I'm delighted for you," I remarked. "If you're truly in love, then I'm happy for you." The smile was back on his face, and I felt better. The last thing I wanted to do was hurt my best friend's feelings. "So tell me all. How did it happen?"

We settled on the stools behind the counter and while we drank coffee, he told me everything. "His name's Doug and we met at the estate sale. It turns out he owns a shop in Kensington, very much like this one. Just think, Cat, we can stock for both stores—after all, we're only about ten minutes away from each other."

I was shocked. "You're already talking about joining forces? Isn't this a bit too soon?"

Scotty rolled his eyes at me. "Oh, darling, it's fate. I'm telling you, Doug's the one!"

I didn't want to dampen his enthusiasm by reminding him he had said the same thing to me a few years back when he first met Mark, so I could only pray this time he had it right. "Well, tell me more," I encouraged him—not that he needed encouragement.

"We have so much in common. It's almost eerie." Scotty explained further, "It turns out he's just gone through a break up, and his ex is a flight attendant, like Mark. I mean, what are the chances, right?"

I could have told him that more than half the men who worked in hospitality and travel were gay, but now was not the time. Besides, Scotty wasn't going to listen to reason, so I let him talk.

"Anyway," he went on, "we just clicked, darling, and one thing led to another and—well, you know."

No, I didn't know, but I could imagine. Scotty was so impulsive when it came to relationships. Still, if he could find true happiness with his newfound love, I wasn't going to be the one to stand in his way. "And?" I prompted.

"Well, we talked late into the night. Doug stayed over, you see."

This was news to me. I must've slept like a log because although I thought I heard Scotty come in, I didn't hear anything else. Of course, my head had been full of Rick and the incredible kiss we shared; so even a meteor could have plunged into the earth, and I wouldn't have been aware of it. Scotty was still talking so I brought my focus back to what he was saying.

"... and he lives alone, so we thought we could move in together for a trial period. What do you think?"

What? I'd missed something important. *Did he just say Doug was moving in with us?* "Scotty, what are you saying?" I exclaimed, my thoughts in chaos. I was already thinking ahead to the possibility of having to move again when I had only just moved in.

Scotty read my mind. "Cat, I'm saying Doug's going to move in with me. We think life's too short to waste any more time when we know we're meant to be. But I don't want you to think you have to go anywhere. I want you to live with us."

I sighed. "Scotty, this is really sweet of you, but you know it won't work. If you and Doug decide to have a life together, I don't want to be in the way." I added, "Our friendship's very important to me, and I think being the third person in your household would have a detrimental effect on it. Besides, you and Doug will need time to settle in as a couple."

Scotty glanced at me with eyes that held something like guilt mixed with love. "I'm so sorry, darling. I feel like such a heel doing this to you now, but I never thought I'd meet someone so soon."

I gave him a reassuring smile. "It's okay. You know what they say about 'the best laid plans' and all that. Hey, maybe your friend's studio's still vacant," I remarked, hoping Scotty's gallery owner friend hadn't let out the place to anyone else. But from the look on Scotty's face, I knew it was wishful thinking. Low cost rentals in this area were snapped up immediately.

"The studio's already gone," Scotty confirmed my thoughts, "but leave it to me. I'll find you something in the area. I have heaps of contacts, and it's the least I can do. In the meantime, however, you're staying with us, and I won't take no for an answer."

"Very well." I gave in to his plans—after all, I had no alternative right now. "But only for a couple of weeks at most," I pointed out.

Scotty placed our cups in the office sink and came back with a notepad and pen. "Okay. Now that we've settled the housing situation, we need to plan my 'end of grief party'," he announced.

"Your what?" What more was he up to now?

He saw the look on my face and was quick to reassure me. "Sorry, darling. I meant the Christmas party I throw for my clients every year. It's almost November, and I want to make sure we do something before people start to plan their holidays."

"What's that got to do with this 'end of grief' thing?" I enquired.

"Well, I thought seeing as I met Doug, I can celebrate twice: Christmas with my clients and a farewell to the grief over Mark, the bitch. Now, help me put together a theme," he declared and started to scribble notes in the notepad. "I was thinking about Villa Caprese, the Italian place at Milsons Point. And for the theme, a Pierrot and Columbine thing with a Venetian *carnivale* setting. What do you think?"

I didn't need to reply; Scotty was already engrossed in writing ideas for his theme party, and I was left feeling like the foolish Pierrot who, according to the story, suffered from unrequited love while Columbine was in love with Harlequin. Only in my situation, the sex of the characters was reversed: I was Pierrot, the lovesick country boy; Denise was Harlequin, the heroic and manly figure who could perform amazing feats; and Rick was Columbine, the beautiful heroine who fell for Harlequin.

Doug moved in a week later, and I fell in love with him. He was the gentlest soul I had ever met, and he instantly became a father figure. Even Henry, who was a very choosy cat, crawled onto his lap the first time we watched TV together, and there he stayed for the duration of the movie.

At forty-four, with a tall and solid frame, green eyes, and salt-and-pepper hair, Doug was nothing like I had imagined him to be.

Judging from Scotty's last relationship, I'd expected another version of Mark: extreme good looks, athletic body, and fussy about clothes—every gay man's dream. In contrast, Doug possessed a kindly face and looked to be a homey type with loose-fitting clothes that, while not stylish, lent him a look of casual elegance. Further, it was his air of calm and gentleness that had the power to draw people to him. I detected strength and wisdom underneath Doug's amiable exterior, and this gave him the kind of confidence others would find attractive. Scotty had obviously felt this, and now, it was me.

Despite this, I still had every intention of finding my own place to live. Much as I loved having Doug around, and discussing all sorts of things with him—even relationships—I knew Scotty only too well. He would want their privacy, and I wanted to have mine. Though now it wasn't urgent any longer that I move out because Doug was such a nice man. Had he been another guy like Mark, I would've gone to stay in a hotel if need be. Mark was opinionated and belittling of anyone of whom he didn't approve, including me; and he had a temper to boot. I still couldn't understand what Scotty had ever seen in him.

The boys tried to change my mind about moving out, and though I remained adamant we finally reached a compromise. I would stay on until the New Year, only a couple of months away, and then I would let Scotty find a suitable place for me. So with this agreement firmly in place, we got down to planning the Christmas function for Scotty's clients.

"I think we should include your clients, too, Dougy," Scotty suggested one evening while we sat around the kitchen table, putting together the invitation list.

"It makes sense," I agreed, and had to smile at Scotty's diminutive of Doug's name. "There's no point in having two parties, is there?"

Doug looked at us with serene eyes. "While I agree it makes sense, I don't want to take the attention away from your business, Scotty. We could always have another function once we announce the merging of the two shops."

This was a far better suggestion, and Scotty agreed while I sighed with inward relief. Doug had Scotty's best interests at heart, and I was now sure that merging the two shops could only be a success.

When Scotty had first mentioned it to me, I'd been quite

concerned, but at the time I hadn't yet met Doug. I was naturally afraid of the possibility Scotty might lose his business after the many years of hard work he'd put into it, cultivating the impeccable reputation Sheppard's Antiques now enjoyed. Now, I was happy for the boys and knew their mutual love for what they did would only bring them closer.

"Okay, so it's settled then," Scotty said. "We'll have another party in the next few months to announce the merger. Meanwhile, you guys have to help me with this list. I have over two hundred people here and I need to trim it down by at least fifty if we want to avoid being overcrowded."

"May I take a look?" I asked, and Scotty passed the list over to me while Doug went to make coffee. I cast my eye down the list of names quickly, and two of them jumped out at me. I remained calm when I remarked, "Scotty, how come you're inviting partners?"

"What do you mean?" he uttered, looking to where I was pointing. "Oh, Rick and Denise." I nodded, resisting the urge to scratch out both names with the pen Scotty still held in his hand. "Well, Denise is also a client," Scotty added. "She's bought plenty of stuff for their home."

Their home? Rick and Denise's home? So it was true, then. They *were* still living as man and wife. My heart contracted in pain, but I forced myself to smile. "Oh, I'm sorry. I didn't know."

I noticed Doug cast me a look of concern. He had obviously picked up on something Scotty had not. "Will you excuse me for a moment? I need to go to the bathroom." I made my escape before Doug had a chance to ask me what was going on. Though we had spoken of relationships in general, I never told him about my feelings for Rick; but in his wisdom, I knew Doug could read my energy—the energy of unrequited love.

126

CHAPTER 17

Scotty booked the entire restaurant and had it decked out in all manner of Venetian-style décor. The place was filled with crystal chandeliers and mirrors—all of them borrowed from the shops of colleagues who specialised in Venetian glassware. There was a vast array of Venetian masks hanging from the walls amidst folds of heavy forest-green velvet curtains. The round dining tables, with sitting capacity for ten guests, were set with Venetian glassware and crockery; and the centrepiece at each table consisted of an elaborate Renaissance-style candelabra decked out with six white candles.

The candlelight bounced off the lavishly mirrored room, creating the glittering effect of an Italian *palazzo*. The finishing touch was added by a group of miming artists dressed in Pierrot, Columbine and Harlequin costumes, who moved about the room entertaining guests with their antics.

The dress code for the evening was formal with a touch of flair, and though most of the guests came in evening dress, some decided to add a domino mask or an elaborate Venetian headdress depicting the style worn during the Renaissance.

As hosts for the evening, the boys wore simple but elegant tuxedos; and much to my delight, I wore a stunning off-the-shoulder floor-length red chiffon gown the boys had given me as a gift. The gown had a delicately embroidered bodice and yards of skirt flowing from a nipped-in waist. It was a dream gown, something a person would have worn to a palace ball, and since Scotty had recreated a little bit of a Renaissance *palazzo*, it suited the occasion perfectly.

"You look truly stunning," whispered Doug in my ear, "and if this Rick fellow doesn't sweep you into his arms and make violent love to you, I'll eat my hat—even though I'm not wearing one." He smirked at the last bit of his comment.

Despite exhilarating visions of Rick making wild, passionate love to me, I managed to laugh at Doug's remark. "Maybe you should go and find a hat," I quipped.

Doug kissed my cheek. "I meant every word I said, dear girl, except for the 'eating my hat' bit."

"Thank you, I really appreciate it." I felt moved by Doug's comment and told myself how blessed I was that aside from Scotty, I had now found another wonderful friend in Doug.

"Hey, you two," Scotty called out and gently nudged his way in between Doug and me. "Stop whispering to each other or I'm going to get jealous."

Doug smiled at him and winked at me. "I'll go and get us a drink while the two of you stand here greeting more of your guests." He left us near the entrance and headed for the bar.

I squeezed Scotty's forearm. "Oh, Scotty, this is so beautiful. I love what you did with the place; and thank you once more for this gown. You're such a lovely and supportive friend."

Scotty kissed me. "And so are you—moving in with me when I needed someone the most, and seeing me through the rough times with Mark. I love you, darling; and now, so does Doug. See? You already have two men eating out of your hand." He made eyes at me, and I laughed merrily.

"Two *gay* men, you mean," I corrected him.

He threw me a saucy smile. "Well, we can't all be perfect, right? But I guess the world would be a lonely place for you women if we didn't have some straight fellows around." He grinned.

I was thoroughly enjoying our jovial banter, but my back stiffened when I saw Rick Blake enter the restaurant with Denise on his arm. He was in a black tux, which made him look sexier than usual—if this was possible—and Denise had on a satin silver-grey gown that hugged her slim figure and accentuated her femininity. She left her dark hair loose and it came just past her slightly tanned shoulders.

I couldn't help but notice the magnificent diamond necklace she wore, which resembled a Victorian fringe-style piece I had recently

128

seen in one of Scotty's Sotheby catalogues.

The necklace was exquisite and packed with sparkling, antique-cut diamonds in a setting of silver-over-yellow gold and with a central drop of around one inch. If memory served me right, there were around twenty carats worth of diamonds in the piece I'd seen in the catalogue; and the piece had been valued at over fifty thousand dollars.

I now wondered if this was the Sotheby's necklace, and whether Rick had Scotty bid for it on his behalf. If so, this was irrefutable proof that Rick and Denise were back together—therefore, he'd had no business kissing me.

"Lovely to see you again, Cat." Rick addressed me like we were mere acquaintances, which we were, minus the one episode where we lost our heads over an extremely passionate kiss. "May I introduce you to Denise Brookley? She's a good client of Scotty's."

Denise shook my hand and gave me a genuine smile. "Lovely to meet you at last, Cat. Rick told me you work with Scotty."

I returned the smile. "It's good to meet you, too, Denise." *Did Rick also tell you he almost made love to me on top of his desk?* I felt my cheeks grow warm, and at that very moment, Doug arrived with Pellegrino water. I could have kissed the man.

Scotty took over and introduced Rick and Denise to Doug while I was left thinking how strange it was that Rick introduced Denise by what I presumed to be her maiden name. He hadn't even mentioned his relationship to her—he simply said she was one of Scotty's clients.

Rick and Denise moved on after exchanging pleasantries with Scotty and Doug, and a group of four people arrived and engaged Scotty in a discussion about certain items he had scouted for them. This kept me from asking Scotty about Rick's rather interesting introduction of Denise *and* the fabulous diamond necklace. I would simply have to wait until I had a moment alone with him.

Meanwhile, I noticed Doug gazing in my direction, a look of fatherly concern on his face. "Out of the two," he announced, "I still think you're the most stunning." And before I could reply, Scotty grabbed Doug's arm and pulled him gently into his circle of clients so he could make introductions.

I moved away from them and went to sit at our table. Most of the guests had arrived by now, and Scotty certainly didn't need me to hang around to greet them. Besides, I hardly knew any of his clients. These were people who rarely came into the shop. They mostly talked with Scotty by phone or over lunch. This was how the well-to-do did business.

While I waited for the first course to be served, I spotted Rick and Denise, who were seated at a table near the expansive windows overlooking the harbour. The lighting in the restaurant had been turned down to a more intimate level and people's voices dropped along with it. From where I sat, it looked like the reunited couple did not have any problems with it. They were conversing with heads close together, smiles on their faces. The little green monster in me reared its ugly head, but I had to push him down and out of the way. I purposely pasted a smile on my face when I caught Rick glancing in my direction, but all the time, rage was eating me up inside. *How dared he assault me with passionate kisses one second and then play it so cool the next?*

I looked away from him as Doug came to the table followed by Scotty and seven other guests, which made the full complement for our seating arrangements. I felt relieved Rick and Denise were not sitting with us. It was bad enough being in the same room, let alone having to socialise with them during dinner. I had Doug on one side of me and Scotty on the other, and being flanked by them gave me the strength I needed to get through the evening.

The dinner was superb. We started with slices of melon wrapped in prosciutto, and a salad of thinly sliced fennel and artichoke, marinated in lemon juice and extra virgin olive oil, with slivers of shaved parmesan. For mains, guests had a choice of roasted deboned duck with sautéed broccoli, garlic and chilli or grilled veal rolled with spinach, nutmeg, and parmesan, drizzled with olive oil. The main course came with side dishes of radicchio salad in a balsamic dressing and a variety of lightly sautéed mushrooms in butter sauce. For those who had room after this feast, there was tiramisu cake, a large choice of miniature Italian pastries, and fresh fruit.

By the time I was having my espresso, I felt stuffed and didn't think I would be able to move. Scotty had organised an orchestra to play both contemporary and traditional Italian love songs, and the dance floor filled up fairly quickly—the guests obviously eager to dance off some of the calories they had consumed. I espied Rick dancing with Denise, but before I had time to brood on this, I was whisked onto the dance floor by Scotty.

"It's a wonderful party, Scotty," I told him as we danced to the slow tempo of a traditional Italian song.

"I'm relieved it's all going extremely well. The food was divine, darling. Don't you think?" Scotty sounded happy.

"Yes, it certainly was divine," I replied, "and so is the whole theme. It was a great idea." I was itching to ask him about Denise's diamond necklace, but didn't have the heart to bring up a subject that might spoil the evening—at least for me. I was sure Scotty would have told me if he'd acquired the necklace at Sotheby's for Rick to give to Denise. But now that I had the chance, I found I really didn't want to ask him.

I danced with various men after Scotty, and within an hour I was exhausted—not to mention the fact that my high heels were killing my feet. I went back to the table and was grateful when a waiter poured me a cooling glass of Pellegrino. Through the crowd, I noticed Rick dancing with an old lady sporting blue-rinsed hair while Denise was with a rather attractive man who looked to be in his late thirties.

I still wondered where the necklace had come from even though I passed up the opportunity to ask Scotty. Perhaps, Denise had purchased it for herself, the thought occurred to me in a flash of inspiration. Hadn't Rick said she was a customer of Scotty's? So I could be making a mountain out of a molehill.

"Care to dance?" I was startled by Rick's smooth voice. Close up, he was more attractive than I could remember, and I was glad I was sitting down because an image of our wild kiss flashed into my mind's eye, and I knew my legs would have never supported me. I hated it that the man had this effect on my limbs.

"I'm rather tired now," I stated, trying to look as if I didn't care one way or the other whether I danced with him. Besides, I wanted him to realise that had he asked me earlier, I might have accepted his invitation, but now I was too tired to bother.

Rick took a seat next to me, draping an arm along the backrest of my chair. "We need to talk," he said in a low voice, close to my ear.

I smelled his wonderful aftershave and almost swooned toward him, but I managed to hold myself rigid. "I have nothing to say. Please go back to your partner. The dance is over and she'll be looking for you." *Ouch! That was a bit bitchy, Cat. If you keep acting like*

131

this, the man will figure out you're madly in love with him.

Rick sighed with frustration. "You still won't let me explain about Denise, will you?"

I ignored his remark and had a sip of water while I smiled at a couple of guests who passed by the table on their way to the dance floor. Just then, I felt the grip of strong fingers around my wrist. I tried to pull away without making a scene, but it didn't work.

"Let go of me!" I uttered in a harsh whisper, still holding a smile on my face for the benefit of anyone watching.

"Come outside," he suggested gently. "We need to talk."

I shook my head. "Actually, I'm about to leave," I informed him. "So if you would kindly let go, I'll be on my way."

"I'll take you home," he offered, still holding onto my wrist. "I know you came here with Scotty, and he's going to stick around for a while yet."

"I was going to catch a taxi," I responded.

"On a Friday night in Sydney? Good luck," Rick replied. And then, "Let me drive you home, please."

It was close to eleven, and I knew there was very little chance I would find a taxi easily. Fridays and weekends were the busiest of times for cabs, and I berated myself for not having had the foresight to book one in advance.

"Oh, all right then," I conceded, not very graciously. "But what about Denise?"

"Don't worry about Denise," Rick assured me, letting go of my wrist and standing up with me. "Come on."

132

CHAPTER 18

We drove back to Scotty's place in silence. I quickly glanced at Rick's profile, but the serious look of concentration he wore while focusing on the road gave nothing away. I tried to imagine what it would be like to be loved by him and was surprised to discover that when compared to Josh, a relationship with Rick would be both nurturing and complete. The revelation took my breath away.

What I used to believe regarding my so-called love for Josh had simply turned out to be a feeling of mutual lust and nothing else. Josh was selfish, self-centred, and only cared about superficial things like the best places to eat, the most expensive hotels to stay in, the best clothes to wear, and the list went on. At the time, I'd thought he was a classy guy, but now I realised he was merely keeping up an image of success, which he didn't feel deep down inside himself. For Josh, life revolved around having the right house in the right suburb with the right things and the right partner; all props to keep up his façade of success.

I now acknowledged that when I gave up my freelancing gig at the magazine in order to write my book, I had somehow diminished my image according to his standards. Freelancing for a glamorous magazine felt much more 'successful' in his estimation than writing a book, which I had every intention to self-publish after my idea had been rejected by a number of publishing houses. This, in Josh's eyes, had probably reduced me to a lesser person—plus the part-time job at Scotty's shop hadn't helped. It would've been something altogether different if I had owned the business, but working for someone else, simply made me a sales assistant; and Josh could not be seen with a mere sales assistant. This explained the transfer of his affections to Elise, the junior partner at his firm.

I had been heartbroken at his infidelity but now, when I thought about it, I found I felt nothing whatsoever for the man. More importantly, my love for Rick stood out like a beacon. This kind of love was founded on the fact that we were equals. We had things in common, and yes, the lust was very strong; but there was also a sense of companionship I had never experienced with Josh. Rick seemed like a rock—he was strong and confident, and he took his responsibilities seriously. The interesting thing was that I hadn't known him long, and I still didn't know what was going on with Denise, but one thing I did know—and this, I put down to women's intuition—if I ended up with Rick, he would never let me down. He had substance, and this was something Josh, for all his taste and sophistication, sadly lacked.

I believed in life you had to experience what you didn't want in order to know what you did want. It was a shame it had taken me five years with Josh to finally figure out I could never love him because he had no substance. I wanted a love I could depend on through thick and thin, and I knew in my heart Rick was a man who would stick by the woman he loved.

Of course, this didn't make things better for me at present. There was still the matter of Denise; and I wondered why it was so difficult for me to believe Rick would waste my time if he was still with her. The behaviour did not seem consistent with his character, I was sure. But I'd been hurt too much in order to trust so easily, and as Shakespeare said: "Therein lies the rub."

"We're here," Rick announced, interrupting my train of thought.

I took the keys out of my bag and we went inside the house. Henry was sleeping on the sofa, but upon seeing us enter, he jumped to the floor and came bounding straight to Rick. *Hmm.* Henry had been a good judge of character when Doug came into the household, so I hoped his cat instincts were right this time as well. Rick bent down to stroke him, and I headed for the kitchen.

"Coffee?" I asked.

Rick nodded. "That'll be great, thanks."

I put on the Bialetti espresso maker with enough ground coffee for two cups and watched Rick and Henry while I waited for the coffee to brew. Rick had taken off his jacket and was in his shirtsleeves, patting Henry's tummy while the big cat rolled on his back and purred with pleasure. Well, he had definitely passed the "Henry" test, and this said a lot more for him than my Man Eligibility Scale.

I heard the coffee begin to bubble into the top chamber of the espresso maker and switched off the stove. We sat on the sofa with our espressos, and Henry tried to climb onto Rick's lap, but I shooed him away. The cat threw me a disdainful glare and then flopped down at Rick's feet where he proceeded to start grooming himself.

"He's a wonderful cat," Rick commented. "I used to have one just like him as a child."

I couldn't imagine Rick with a cat. For some reason he struck me as more of a dog person. Perhaps, it was because he exuded such masculinity that I had a difficult time imagining him with a fussy cat.

Rick savoured the coffee for a few moments and then turned to me. "About Denise," he stated, and I tensed, "it's not what you think."

"And what do I think?" I threw him a challenging look.

"There's nothing between us, I assure you." He sounded as though he was trying to placate me, and despite my resolve to stay calm and hear him out, the image of that gorgeous necklace popped into my mind and I couldn't get past it.

"Did Scotty buy the necklace on your behalf?" It was out of my mouth before I could stop it.

Rick gave me a puzzled look. "What necklace? What are you talking about?"

"The necklace Denise is wearing tonight," I blurted out. I might as well go all the way now, I decided.

Understanding suddenly dawned on Rick's face, and he smiled. "Oh, yes. I gave it to her, but—"

"So you don't even deny it!" I threw at him. "You know what? I don't want to hear about Denise. No man spends fifty thousand dollars on a gift for an ex-wife."

"Cat, you still don't understand, and you won't let me finish explaining, damn it!" He went to reach for my hand, but I moved it out of the way and stood up.

"Look, it's not my business after all. I know what I see; and to me, it seems things are not over between you and Denise. So I'm not

135

about to get involved with a man who—"

"My God, why can't you be quiet for once?" He moved with lightning speed, and somehow I was in his arms with his mouth on mine.

Despite the protests with my fists hitting against his chest, he kissed me deeply. I couldn't break the embrace, but let's face it—I wasn't trying very hard. We kissed for a long time, and when we came up for air, I lay on the sofa with Rick on top of me. He looked deep into my eyes, and I wanted to drown in the chocolate brown of his; but just as quickly as he had pulled me into his arms, he was up off the sofa and helping me to my feet.

"I'm sorry. I don't know what it is about you, but whenever you're around, I lose my head. This won't happen again."

I straightened my dress and readjusted the bodice, which had ridden rather low over my breasts. "I think it's best if you leave," I declared though in my heart I wanted him to stay. "After my last relationship, I'm afraid I can't trust that easily; and I have no wish to be lied to again."

Rick's face reflected anger and his eyes seemed to cut into me. "I was not about to lie to you, but if you don't want to hear what I have to say, then I'll leave you to draw your own conclusions," his voice was firm, and I instantly regretted my stupid behaviour. I should at least let him explain although I truly didn't know what possible explanation he could give for purchasing such an expensive piece of jewellery for his ex.

Rick put on his jacket and made his way to the door. "I'm sorry about tonight. It was obviously a mistake." Before I could say anything, he walked out, shutting the door behind him rather firmly.

"Oh!" I cried out in frustration and was rewarded by a curious glance from Henry. "Cat, you're an idiot!" I reprimanded myself.

Rick had been prepared to explain everything, and I had to go and sabotage the whole thing because I was afraid of trusting. Yes, I was afraid, I admitted to myself. Afraid that perhaps I'd made a mistake, and Rick was not as noble as I thought him to be; and if I ended up with him only to go through the same thing I experienced with Josh? I plopped down on the sofa and cried. *Cat, when are you going to learn not to jump to conclusions?*

Christmas came, and we closed the shop until the first week of January. Sydney was dead during this time of year with most people going on vacation, preferably to somewhere cooler.

Scotty and Doug fussed over me and roped me into trimming the tree and drinking cold eggnog laced with lots of brandy. They cooked a scrumptious turkey, even though it was as hot as an oven in the city and a traditional turkey dinner was the last thing we needed.

We did, however, eat out on the terrace under a sky studded with brilliant stars and with the lightest of breezes blowing in from the Pacific Ocean, which was not too far from where we lived.

After my disastrous parting from Rick, I didn't see him again—and though he sent a Christmas hamper along with a card to Scotty's shop, he addressed the card to "Scotty and friends". I kept hoping he would drop by the shop on some pretext, but he stayed away, and while the boys tried to cheer me up, my spirits still flagged.

I had recounted the whole tale to them the day after the party, leaving out the passionate kiss, and though they were sympathetic, there wasn't much they could do in order to lighten my mood.

"Cat, I know this isn't the time to say it, but you know you always jump to conclusions far too quickly," Scotty pointed out gently.

"You're right, Scotty," I replied, and he looked at me with pride in his eyes just before I added, "This isn't the time to say it!"

Scotty burst into laughter. "Sorry, darling," he apologised, "but I thought you were finally going to admit you let your half-Irish temper get the better of you."

"Well, you thought wrong." I grinned, but I acknowledged I was impulsive and often jumped to conclusions without thinking things through. This often got me into trouble, but it was my nature and I couldn't help it.

Doug patted my shoulder. "Don't let it worry you right now, Cat. Perhaps, things will look up in the New Year. Just give it time, dear girl."

Doug was sweet, and I was grateful once again I had the two boys looking out for me. Despite my low spirits, we managed to have a lovely Christmas. When New Year's Eve came around, the boys were invited to a party on someone's yacht to watch the fireworks on Sydney Harbour. They declined, opting to stay home with me. This was so nice of them, it made me cry. We stayed up until midnight and toasted in the New Year together, and I consoled myself with the fact that I had my family around me.

The question of my moving out hadn't come up anymore, but a few days into the New Year, I brought it up with Scotty.

"Darling, all my contacts are away on holidays at the moment. Besides, Doug and I are going away for a week. We decided to combine a small break with a business trip, and we're off to Vietnam. Doug's got contacts over there and we're going to be shopping for some very nice pieces," he informed me. "So you'll have the house to yourself, and Henry will keep you company."

I smiled. "Well, as long as Henry's here with me, then everything's okay."

Scotty regarded me closely. "Is that a real smile or are you putting it on for my benefit?"

"It's real enough, Scotty," I assured him. "I won't deny I don't regret what happened with Rick, but I have to get on with my life. I'm going to start working on my book again, which has been gathering dust all this time. And the rest of the time, I'll run the shop for you when you need me."

"Well, it's certainly great to hear you're sounding more positive," Scotty remarked.

"Like I said, I have to get on with things." I then changed the subject to more practical matters. "I take it you'll want me at the shop while you're away?"

Scotty nodded, and we talked for a while about expected shipments and deliveries for me to arrange. "And I promise, darling," Scotty added, "that as soon as we're back I'll find you somewhere nice to live."

"Somewhere affordable, you mean," I corrected him.

He grinned. "That, too."

The boys left for their trip the day before I was due to re-open the shop, and I settled into a routine while they were away. By day, I attended to the shop, and in the evenings I resumed work on my book.

The dating blog ran itself insofar as readers sharing their dating stories, and as moderator I made sure we always had plenty of discussion threads. As long as I kept busy, I had little time to think of Rick, and this was the way I liked it. Between the work at the shop and my writing, I was tired enough that usually, after an early dinner, I often fell asleep on the sofa with Henry while we watched golden oldies.

I realised it was going to take some time for me to get over the whole situation with Rick, but at least I was now making headway.

CHAPTER 19

Despite my intentions to get over Rick, I became more and more restless in my routine as the week wore on, and I found work alone wasn't going to do it. It didn't help that Scotty and Doug were not around and I was stuck with only Henry for company. Much as I loved my gentle furry companion, I couldn't settle into anything. I wasn't doing much writing, either, except for keeping an eye on the blog threads. I was at a loose end and didn't know what to do.

One evening, after a particularly moving golden oldie, I switched off the TV and went online to kill time. I checked the blog, and one of the threads caught my attention.

"If you fall off the horse, get right back on it," it read. Feeling curious, I went into the discussion forum. The first post was about a woman, Cynthia, who had been dating for some time and things were going really well; so much so, that she was on the point of moving in with the guy.

As she was making preparations to move, however, she saw him one day lunching with another woman, and looking rather intimate. When she confronted him about it, she found out he was already married to the lady in question. It turned out he had done this before, keeping two households at once. I quickly read some of the responses to this poor woman's predicament.

AnnieB
Oh, Cynthia, are you saying he admitted to keeping two households? How horrendous for you.

140

Cynthia

At least, I found out in time. But yes, it was horrendous. It was painful, and I felt used and betrayed. I'm only grateful I didn't move in with him. The woman in the relationship before I became involved with him had two kids—and this guy has kids of his own. Can you believe it? I was really upset for a while and stopped looking around, but then I thought if I didn't go on dating other men, this creep would've won. Guys like this should be jailed.

LostForLove

I totally agree about the jail bit. These bastards would sure think twice before playing around with other people's feelings. Good on you, Cynthia, for moving on.

MissGlitter

I had something similar happen to me, only difference was this guy had not two, but three households! Of course, he was rich and could afford it, but he wasn't married to any of us. Imagine his surprise when it turned out that we all knew each other (as we belonged to the same gym), and we figured out we were all living with the same guy. His occupation of business executive was really convenient because he was supposedly "away" for part of the time on business trips. This was how he divided his time among us.

One night, the three of us got together at my place (it was his turn to stay with me), and when he came home from work, we really let him have it. I think the he thought we'd turned into the Witches of Eastwick. We threw everything we could think of at him: pots, pans, gifts he'd given us—one woman even threw her diamond necklace at him. Needless to say, the guy got out of there as fast as his legs could carry him, but not without some bruises.

The one good thing that came out of this is the three of us became very good friends, and we were able to support each other through the emotional upheaval that followed. So from now on, every time we meet a new guy for a date, we check with each other to make sure we aren't seeing the same man.

I couldn't read any more, and I shut the lid of my laptop rather forcefully. A diamond necklace! The guy had given one of the women a diamond necklace—and he was keeping three women at once. The nerve of him! I tried not to think of Denise, especially about becoming friends with her only to find out both of us were seeing the same man. God forbid!

The one thing I liked, though, was Cynthia's comment about getting out there once again, despite what had happened. This must have taken a lot of courage, and the woman had been a lot closer than I to being in a full-on relationship with the guy.

The idea was tantalising—and I remembered saying I might give internet dating a go if I became desperate. Well, I *was* desperate. I was close to forty years of age, single, and with a significant relationship behind me that hadn't worked out. My chances of finding someone new were probably zilch, but there wasn't anything preventing me from trying to get back on the saddle and have some fun.

Suddenly, I thought of David. He'd been one of the nicest guys I had met through the net, but I wasn't going to use his feelings for me to assuage my own. No. I must start afresh and simply go out on different dates for fun. If anything should come of it, then it would be a bonus.

It was too early to go to bed, so I made coffee and went back online. I signed into *Let's Meet* and edited my profile, changing my photo to a more recent one, plus I added more to my blurb. This time, I was going to date for real.

Within minutes of updating my profile, I had five "Let's meet" requests. The first three were not my cup of tea, but the last two had possibilities, especially one that went by the name of LoveActually. I tried him first.

The guy was handsome, according to his photo. In fact, he reminded me a little of David, with the dark hair and boyish face. He worked in finance, was thirty-eight, never married, widely travelled, loved art, non-smoker, and lived in the eastern suburbs. Wow, this was getting better and better. Before I changed my mind, I replied to his request and suggested a meeting at Lorenzo's in two days' time. LoveActually happened to be online and we chatted for a while, agreeing to the meeting. His real name was James.

We met as arranged, and I was impressed. James epitomised the cliché of tall, dark, and handsome, but with a certain exotic look adding to his allure. He wore jeans, accentuating a well-built, athletic frame, and a white shirt showing off a light tan. His eyes were a mix between hazel and amber, and they held a bit of a wicked gleam I found rather attractive.

142

I was glad I had taken the trouble to look presentable in a white cotton Indian skirt with a matching three-quarter sleeve blouse and tan Roman-style sandals. I wore a few silver bangles and long silver drop earrings with a Celtic-looking design.

It was too hot for cappuccinos, so we ordered iced coffees. We had much in common and talked and talked as the afternoon flew by. A few hours later, we were still at the café and on to our third drink.

"I'm all coffeed out," I declared, and we laughed.

His attractive eyes took me in and for a moment, I thought of Henry's amber eyes. James's eyes were almost the exact same colour. "Me, too," he uttered. "So what now?"

A little warning bell inside my head told me to call it a day. I would've loved to have moved on to dinner with him, but I didn't want to run the risk of going too fast. Besides, I wanted to see if he would call me back. If he did, then I would know he was truly interested and not just passing the time.

"I had a great afternoon, James, but I need to get back now. Perhaps, I'll see you online," I remarked casually. This would ensure he didn't see me as being too desperate.

James smiled rather charmingly and his eyes gave me a playful look. "Oh, I'll definitely see you online, but I would rather make a time to meet with you again right now, if you don't mind. I'd love to have dinner with you."

Wow! He obviously didn't need time to think about it. The man liked me, and I couldn't believe my luck at having met someone who was not only good looking, but with whom I had so much in common.

"That would be nice," I replied, feeling a little shy all of a sudden.

We made arrangements to meet at Frangipani on Friday evening, and I went home with stars in my eyes. I couldn't believe how easy it had been. Like Cynthia from the blog, I was back in the saddle and about to have lots of fun.

Even though the rest of the week was frantic with customers, and deliveries and shipments arriving at the shop, Friday was slow to come. By the afternoon, I was tired but excited at the prospect of my date with James.

I closed the shop promptly at five and rushed home to feed Henry and have a shower. James was meeting me at seven-thirty so I had plenty of time in which to rest and pick out my wardrobe.

I decided to wear the Lisa Ho buff and mocha outfit, which consisted of a buff-coloured close-fitting skirt that clung to my hips and went to just above the knee, and a short cotton jacket of the same colour with a couple of bone buttons. Under the jacket, I wore a sleeveless, mocha knit top, and I set off the outfit with medium-heeled, sand-coloured slingback pumps in woven canvas. I wore a minimum of jewellery, which I borrowed from the shop. This consisted of a gorgeous antique beaten-gold bangle with a pair of matching earrings. The effect looked somewhat Egyptian, and it suited the outfit perfectly.

James was waiting for me outside the restaurant when I arrived a few minutes after our appointed time. "Sorry," I apologised. "Friday night traffic."

He looked cool in a pair of bone-coloured tailored pants and a black silk shirt. "I've only just arrived myself," he said and pecked my cheek. He then motioned me inside the restaurant. "How come you drove anyway? I thought you lived in Paddington."

"I've been standing at work all day, so I thought it best to drive," I replied.

What I told him was not entirely true. Despite the fact that we had clicked right from the start, it didn't mean I was going to trust him so quickly. I had to get to know him a little better first, and having my own car was my means of escape in the event things didn't work out.

The restaurant was jam-packed, but James had booked ahead and we were shown to an intimate corner table, located on the restaurant's back deck and overlooking an exotic garden filled with the fragrance of frangipani and star jasmine. The atmosphere was intoxicating, and I felt as though I was in the tropics instead of the heart of Sydney.

"This is very nice, isn't it?" I commented as a waitress in traditional Thai dress brought the menus.

James gazed at me from across the candlelit table. "*You're* very nice," he responded as he reached for my fingers and gave them a light caress.

I pretended not to notice and made a show of picking up the menu and studying it like they were going to give us an exam on it. Meanwhile, I regretted that the top I was wearing underneath my

144

jacket was sleeveless and fitted snuggly against my body. I felt hot in the jacket but didn't want to take it off in case James saw this as a come-on. I could see I was going to have to tread carefully.

We took a few minutes over the menu and finally ordered. When the waitress asked about drinks, I ordered a Pellegrino water while James asked for white wine. "You're not drinking?" he asked while the waitress waited with her pen poised over the order pad.

"No, thank you." I smiled toward the waitress to signify we needed nothing else. The girl nodded and walked off to fill our order.

"How come you don't want wine?" James insisted, once again reaching for my fingers.

I moved my hand away from his by pretending I was adjusting the serviette on my lap. "I don't always drink," I replied. "Isn't this a great garden?" I added, trying to divert his attention, but his eyes remained on my face, which was starting to feel very warm.

"You look beautiful tonight," his voice was smooth as his eyes devoured me. "You're intoxicating."

I squirmed in my chair and wished the waitress would hurry with our drinks. I had to have some water to cool off and was glad I ordered a non-alcoholic drink because I now knew I was going to need all my wits about me to parry James's advances.

It was obvious I had made a big mistake in agreeing to have dinner with him so soon, but I was relieved I brought my car so I could drive away the minute dinner was over. I failed to understand how I could have misjudged James. Our first meeting had gone so well, and he had made no advances toward me except for being rather charming. But now, he gazed at me like I was his possession.

Thankfully, the drinks arrived, and I launched into a big discussion about art and antiques. Whenever James tried to pay me a compliment, I ignored it and brought up another topic for discussion. And this was how I made it through dinner.

By the time we finished eating, I was exhausted by all the topics I'd touched upon: Renaissance art, antique furniture, the sometimes dodgy world of art dealers, the latest Sotheby's auction and the prices certain items fetched, and the list went on. When our coffees arrived, I was pretty much out of material, and I finally knew how stand-up comedians felt in front of a difficult audience, trying to keep them amused for a couple of hours.

Glancing at my watch, I noted it was only after nine, but I

couldn't take it anymore. I had to get away. "I had a lovely time tonight, James," I announced, "but I have to work tomorrow, and need to get some rest."

James gazed at me for the longest time, a silly smile on his face—undoubtedly brought on by the bottle of wine he consumed on his own. "You know, you are very beautiful," he stated, leaning across the table so his face was closer to mine. "I'd like to come home with you and make love."

The thought repulsed me, and so did his alcohol breath. I pushed back my chair and it made a loud, scraping noise noticed by other diners. "Please, James, I really have to go," I told him, and this time I was firm.

James didn't budge, but at least he motioned for the bill to be brought to our table, and waved his hand at me when he saw me reach for my wallet. "Dinner's on me," his voice was still smooth, but it sounded slurred.

I didn't insist on paying. I just wanted to get home as quickly as possible. Finally, when the account was settled, we started to make our way out of the restaurant. As we walked through the dining area toward the exit, I saw Rick seated at a table with the lovely Denise. Our eyes met across the room and it was like time stood still; so much so that I didn't even notice James's hand on the small of my back as he escorted me across the dining room. Then, Denise said something to Rick, and the spell was broken. I looked away and hurried outside with a not-too-steady James close behind me.

"Are you going to be okay driving?" I asked, once out on the sidewalk. The fresh air was a welcome change to the heat inside the restaurant.

James put his arm around my shoulders and whispered in my ear, "Concerned about my welfare, huh? Let me come home with you, then."

I shook free of his hold. "Please, James. This isn't working out. You've had too much to drink, and I'm happy to call you a cab so you get home safely. But you're *not* coming to my place." I was speaking quite firmly, but none of what I said seemed to be getting through to him. I could also feel Rick watching me from his table by the front window, which faced the street, and I didn't want to make a scene in front of him, but it seemed James had other ideas.

"Oh, come on!" he declared rather harshly all of a sudden. "You

146

know you want it." He pulled me to him before I had time to dodge his arms, and his mouth landed on mine as his hand slipped inside the collar of my top and grabbed my breast.

I was sickened by the smell on his breath and his fingers playing with my nipple. I tried to push him away, but he was too strong for me. His kiss was so foul I was sure I was going to bring up my dinner. I thought it would serve him right if I vomited all over him. My primary concern, however, was to get him away from me, and I wasn't having any success. His hand left my breast and slipped past the waistband of my skirt while his mouth was still latched onto mine. I kept pushing, and because I wasn't able to dislodge him, I began to panic.

I managed to pull my mouth away from his, but this only enabled him to hold me in place a lot closer as he locked his chin into my shoulder, making it impossible for me to escape. My arms were pinned between his body and mine, and I felt so helpless for a moment, I thought I was going to faint. By this time, his fingers had found their way into my panties, and he started to feel for the area between my legs. I felt nauseated but managed to yell into his ear, "Let me go!"

Then, suddenly, I was free. I stumbled backward and almost fell into the open door of the restaurant, but a hand shot out and steadied me. Next thing, I saw James on the ground, nursing an eye, which was rapidly swelling, and Rick standing over him, a look of murder on his face.

"You bastard!" James yelled from his supine position, a hand covering his eye. "I'll have you up for charges."

I noticed most the diners in the restaurant were looking our way, but I didn't care. I was relieved Rick had intervened. Denise came out the door, holding a glass of water toward me. "Drink this," she offered, pressing the glass into my hand.

I grabbed it and drank down the cool liquid greedily as I watched Rick pick James up by the scruff of his collar. "You clear out of here right now or it'll be you who'll be charged for drunken disorder and assaulting a lady."

Though he swayed badly, James managed to stand on his feet. Rick was successful in hailing a passing cab; and still holding James by his collar, he pushed him into the waiting car. "Take him home," Rick told the driver through the open window, "and if he can't

147

remember where he lives, take him to the nearest police station." He then drew a few dollar bills from his wallet and handed them to the driver. "This ought to cover the fare." The cab sped off, and Rick made his way back to us.

"Th… thank… you," I stammered to him and Denise. I handed the glass back to her. "I need to go home now."

"Wait," said Rick, "let us drive you there."

Much as I appreciated his help and Denise's kindness, I really couldn't drive back home with them—not when they were together. Not when I loved Rick with all my heart. I simply wanted to go home and shower so I could get James's smell off me and then have a good cry about the whole thing.

"I'm grateful, but my car is just down the street and it's only a two-minute drive. Thank you for helping me. I really appreciate it." I mustered a smile for their benefit. Then, I fled.

CHAPTER 20

I didn't have time to think about the incident with James and the timely rescue by Rick when I arrived home because Scotty and Doug were waiting for me as I walked in. I rushed over to them and gave each a big hug. They were a welcome sight.

"It's so good to have you back, but I didn't expect you until tomorrow," I remarked once we settled in the lounge room.

"I forgot about an estate sale I was supposed to attend," explained Doug. "Ordinarily, I would've let it go, but this particular one has some interesting pieces a good client of mine commissioned, so I had to come back. The sale's on tomorrow."

"And how was the trip?" I asked, showing an enthusiasm I didn't feel right now. I really wanted to shower and go to bed.

Scotty smiled. "It was great, but as usual, too short. We plan to return one of these days. I mean, we had time to conclude our business, but not much for anything else."

This was a great opener for me to bring up my move. It was obvious the boys needed time together to settle into their relationship, and though I loved them dearly, I knew it was also time for me to go. I had stayed a lot longer than I had intended due to Christmas and then the boys going overseas, but now that things were back to normal, I needed to move on.

I also wanted my own place so I could start healing my broken heart. I still couldn't get away from the fact that Rick had been with Denise once again. Despite what he tried to explain about her, I was convinced the two were looking to get back together. Tonight, at the restaurant, they'd looked so cosy together I couldn't fathom any other explanation that justified the two being in each other's company so much.

The sight of them talking intimately had affected me to the point that I had temporarily forgotten James, the lecher. And if it hadn't been for the fact that Rick had rescued me, I would have preferred not to have seen him at all. Why was it when you were trying to avoid someone, they kept popping up everywhere? It was obvious the universe loved to play its little tricks on lovesick people.

"You look smashing," Doug remarked, bringing me out of my gloomy thoughts. "Have you been out tonight?"

I nodded and bit my bottom lip, my eyes downcast. "It's not what you think. I didn't go out with Rick." I looked up and saw the boys giving me a sympathetic smile. "In fact, I did something really stupid." I sighed and decided I was going to relate the whole story about my desperation and decision to go on a real internet date. I mentioned this briefly and had their undivided attention. I added, "Before I go into it, though, I need a shower and a cup of tea."

Looks of concern were thrown my way, but the boys didn't say anything. Doug went to make the tea, and Scotty came up to me and gave me a quick hug. "Hurry back."

I scrubbed like mad in the shower and brushed my teeth at least three times before I gargled with extra strength mouthwash. My skin was almost red raw from the loofah I used to scrub off every bit of microscopic matter before I was finally satisfied that I had erased James's germs from me.

I still couldn't believe what an easy target I'd been. The man was a menace, and I intended on reporting him to *Let's Meet* so they would cancel his profile and alert their female members. I wasn't sure whether dating sites had warning systems, but if *Let's Meet* didn't, I was going to post something on my blog. It might not help much, but even if I could help one female from going through this, it would be enough.

When I finished showering, I changed into pyjamas and rejoined the boys. We lounged around on the sofa and had chamomile tea and wafer biscuits while I regaled them with the horror of my experience. When I finished my tale, there was stunned silence in the room for a few moments. Scotty was the first to break it.

"Oh, my God!" he exclaimed in shock. "How awful for you! The guy should be charged with assault, Cat. You need to go to the police, I mean—"

"It's okay, Scotty," I reassured him. "No harm done. If anything, it was disgusting and embarrassing, more than anything else."

"Yes, but he shouldn't be allowed to get away with it," Doug added.

"Perhaps, if Rick hadn't intervened and socked him one in the eye, I might've done something. In any case, I really don't have much to go with. The guy simply had too much to drink and pawed me. I don't think the police would be interested."

"Well, I'm glad Rick punched him out," Scotty declared before sighing. "How romantic!"

I laughed. "I wouldn't exactly call it that. I mean, he was only helping me out. Besides, he was with Denise; and she was nice enough to bring me some water. I felt so helpless about the whole thing." I looked down, trying to hide tears of self-pity.

Scotty moved over to sit next to me and pulled me into his arms. "Well, whatever the case, I'm glad you're okay, darling. In time, you'll be just fine."

"By the way," I quickly wiped away my tears and sat up straight, "you promised you'd help me find a place to live, and now that you're back, I'm going to hold you to it."

Doug cut in before Scotty could reply. "Cat, we don't want you to move out. Things are working out just fine."

"Boys," I stated, throwing them a warning look. "We've been through this once before."

Doug and Scotty sighed in unison. "Okay, darling," Scotty nodded resignedly. "I'll find you something. It's unnecessary, mind, but I'll find you something."

True to his word, within a couple of weeks, Scotty found me a lovely little studio in Woollahra, just one street back from Rick's Café. This was too close for comfort, but seeing as the rent was reasonable and I would still be living in an area I liked, I was grateful to take it. Secretly, I prayed I wouldn't run into Rick.

The studio was above a quaint gift store located in a rustic sandstone building, and the owner, who was a friend of Scotty's, was happy to have me live there as I came highly recommended. The place was roomier than where I used to rent and it was squeaky clean with a new kitchenette, inclusive of dishwasher and ample light coming in from windows facing the street below. The place came unfurnished, but between Scotty and Doug, I ended up with a roomfull of beautiful vintage and antique furniture.

I wanted to pay the boys for everything, but they wouldn't hear of it. They simply clucked around me like mother hens and every time they visited, they brought yet another piece they thought I needed.

It was fun having a place of my own again. Much as I had enjoyed living with the boys, I had privacy now and could grieve for my lost love any time I wanted. I could even have a pity party by watching chick flicks, crying my eyes out, and using huge wads of tissues while I drank red wine to drown my sorrows. I could hang around in my pyjamas all day and eat pizza out of a box or overdose on large pieces of chocolate—all things I couldn't do at Scotty's place.

Scotty would've had a coronary if he saw me eat pizza out of a box! I smiled at the thought. For him, it was civilised restaurants and expensive antiques that did the trick when trying to heal a broken heart.

Once I settled in the new place, I emailed *Let's Meet* to report James. The site administrator responded by informing me they had cancelled his profile. I knew this wouldn't stop James from opening a new one under a different name. Further, *Let's Meet* did not have an alert system, therefore, I posted to my blog, warning women about James, but I couldn't very well use his photo and denounce him as this would be defamation of character, and potentially, he could take action against me. So short of describing his appearance in words, there was nothing much else I could do.

One thing I did do, however, was make the decision not to date on the internet ever again. Dating in order to get over a broken heart was not the right thing to do, and it could even hurt the other person. My short relationship with David was a case in point. The best thing was to give myself time to get over Rick and, in the meantime, get on with my life.

Lola from the magazine rang me in late January to tell me the discussion forums were going so well they had decided to hand the project over to one of their permanent staff members. I was secretly relieved to hear this as I could make more money working at Scotty's, and I wouldn't have to read any more dating stories.

Scotty and Doug merged their businesses, and we were now busier than ever due to the referral of clients from Doug. Basically, the boys had decided to downsize Doug's shop, and Scotty's, being the larger of the two, handled most of the business. Besides, Doug enjoyed attending auctions and estate sales with Scotty more than running his shop. For me, this meant Doug offered additional hours of work at his place in Kensington; and now I divided my time between the two shops. During my free time, I made a start once again on my Renaissance art book.

I was so busy with all my activities that I had little time to think about Rick, and to date I'd been lucky not to bump into him although I had to walk past his place to go to the shops along the main street of Woollahra. I could've driven to Paddington for groceries and other supplies but decided not to hide in order to avoid a chance meeting. I figured if it happened, I would have to cope with it. So it was ironic that instead of bumping into Rick, I actually ended up coming across Denise.

One sunny morning, on my day off, I was walking along the main drag on the way to the small supermarket down the street from Rick's Café when, from across the road, I espied Denise coming out of Rick's with another man.

I was surprised to see her with someone other than Rick, but it was none of my business. I kept walking, but I glanced in her direction a couple of times. She caught my eye before I could look away and waved at me. Then, she crossed the road, her hand in the other man's. She smiled when she reached me.

"Cat, fancy seeing you here," she greeted me in a friendly voice. "How have you been?"

I was a little taken aback that she still remembered my name, having only met me formally at Scotty's Christmas function and then fleetingly at the restaurant on the night of the incident with James.

"Hi Denise," I replied casually. "I live in these parts, having recently moved here from Paddington." I eyed her companion, whose hand she was still holding. He was a tall man, possibly early to mid-forties like Rick. He had a handsome countenance with blue eyes and straight dark hair swept back from his face.

"Oh, how rude of me," Denise remarked when she realised she hadn't made the introduction. "This is my husband, Peter Brookley."

My mouth must have gaped wide open, but she didn't notice

because she turned to the man. "Pete, this is Cat Ryan. She works with Scotty."

Peter took my hand in a firm grip and shook it. "Oh, so you're the Cat Denise told me had to be rescued at the restaurant. Nice to meet you."

I must've looked like a stunned fish, but no one seemed to notice. Taking hold of my arm, Denise asked, "Do you have time for coffee? Rick's always talking about you, but I haven't had a chance to get to know you properly."

If she had said I had a third eye growing out of my forehead, I would've been less surprised. "Oh! Why... yes, of course," I managed to reply.

We walked a couple of doors down from where we were standing and went into Gianni's, a small corner café, which only served coffee and cakes. The place was crowded, but we found a table toward the back of the room and sat down. I still wasn't functioning properly, so I simply followed the others, letting Denise take the lead.

Peter ordered cappuccinos and almond biscotti all around while Denise turned to me and asked, "So how are you after the nasty shock?"

What shock? I wanted to ask—the one with James or this one? I assumed she was referring to the incident with James. "He was just a date," I told her. "And if I'd known he was a drunk, I would've never gone out with him."

"Lucky thing Rick was with me," Denise remarked.

"Yes, very lucky." I was still trying to recover from the shock of Denise being married to Peter. How was it possible when every time I saw her, she was with Rick? And how come she spoke so openly about him when Peter was in our presence? Plus what was that about Rick talking to her about me? Oh, my God, if the woman didn't say anything soon, I was going to go crazy.

We chitchatted a little bit about my work at Scotty's and Denise went into squeals of delight when I mentioned some of the pieces she recognised from having seen them at the shop. Thank God the coffees arrived, giving me something to do with my hands so I wouldn't have to focus too much on my chaotic thoughts.

So far, I hadn't been able to get any information out of Denise that was of any value—except for the wonderful news she was married and, therefore, not getting back together with Rick. After all, one look at the two in front of me, and I could tell they were madly in love with each other. I was dying to know what was going on.

"Don't mind Denise," Peter said after she let out another squeal of delight when I finished describing a French boudoir four-poster bed we had just acquired. "It's the hormones."

Now, I was truly puzzled. Denise was too young to be going through menopause. "The hormones?" I repeated stupidly.

"We're expecting our first child," Peter announced, a big grin on his face.

"Oh, congratulations!" I cried out, feeling elated. Not just for them, but because all my doubts about Rick had just flown out the window.

"Now that we have a family on the way, we're very happy we're not going to lose the house," Denise informed me. "This is why I'm squealing all the time. I'm so happy."

I didn't know what she was talking about. Peter saw the confusion on my face and explained, "We've been renovating a house we purchased a couple of years back. It's an old building, but very grand, which means we needed quite a bit of money to restore it. A few months ago, I was laid off from my job and we thought we were going to lose everything. We were at wits' end; especially after Denise found out she was pregnant."

Denise had been all smiles while Peter was speaking, but now she took over. "Rick's been wonderful! He made it possible for us to keep the house, and now Peter has a good job prospect, so things are coming together for us."

I didn't know what to say. I had only met Denise briefly and here she was, opening right up to me and being so friendly. I found I liked her. Of course, it helped to know she wasn't getting back with Rick. Oh, Rick—now I wished I had let him explain!

"I'm very happy for you," I said, and meant it. "But forgive me if I still seem a little unclear. When Rick introduced you at Scotty's party by the name of Brookley, I simply assumed it was your maiden name; so you took me by surprise just now." I couldn't very well ask her why she didn't bring Peter to any of the meetings she'd had with Rick.

Denise laughed, and I couldn't help but admire her exuberant beauty. I wished one day I would look as she did—happy and in love.

155

"Sorry, Cat, you must've thought I was getting back together with Rick." She laughed some more, and Peter joined in.

I felt my cheeks grow warm. She'd hit the nail on the head, but I wasn't going to admit to it. Luckily, Denise and Peter were still laughing at the notion and neither of them noticed my red face.

"Perhaps, I should explain," Denise said finally. "Peter was away visiting his mother for a while. She had some health problems; but she's fine now."

"I'm glad that's the case." I smiled at Peter.

"We were concerned for a while, but everything turned out okay," Peter replied.

"Anyway," Denise took up the thread of the conversation again, "Rick was nice enough to keep me company at the party since Peter was away. We'd been meeting a lot recently about the financial assistance he's giving us, so it was nice to have a social evening for a change. I bet you really thought we were getting back together, huh?" She giggled. "Cat," she took hold of my hand. "I'm fairly sure the man has feelings for you. Rick likes to think he can control his emotions, but I saw the way he looks at you."

If someone at the table had sneezed at that moment, I would have been blown off my chair.

156

CHAPTER 21

I was in two minds as to what to do with my newfound information once I came off cloud nine. On the one hand, I didn't want to stir things up with Rick in case he was no longer interested in me. After all, when I refused to listen to his explanation about Denise, he said he would leave me alone. On the other hand, if I didn't do something, I was going to lose him. Denise thought Rick had a thing for me, and the fact he told her so much about me lent weight to her opinion.

Rick was a man of his word, and I knew he would leave me alone as he promised. So if I didn't do anything about the situation, we would eventually become acquaintances who'd exchange polite conversation if we happened to run into each other. It seemed the ball was in my court. I now knew Rick was not getting together with Denise, and he liked me. The only problem was I didn't have any idea how to approach him. I could brazenly walk into his café and ask to see him in private or I could go see him under some pretext or other. I decided on the pretext.

I telephoned Scotty in the early afternoon after my coffee with Peter and Denise. "Do you need anything to be delivered to Rick's?" I asked casually.

"It's your day off, so what's going on?" Scotty sounded suspicious.

"Why should there be anything going on? I only thought Rick might need something delivered to him," I remarked in an off-hand manner.

A pause and then, "Why can't this wait until you're back in the morning? Cat, this is Scotty talking to you, not a gullible five-year-old."

I sighed. "All right, I'll tell you." I couldn't lie to Scotty, he saw through me far too easily, so I told him about the chance meeting with Denise and all that had transpired.

"Wow!" he exclaimed. "That's certainly a huge turn of events. I take it you're still madly in love with him." This was a statement, not a question. I was obviously very transparent.

"Yes, I am in love with him," I confessed, "but I guess I'm too scared to find out whether or not he feels the same way. You see my predicament, don't you? I can't just go there and tell him I changed my mind and that I now believe him about Denise."

"Why not?"

"Scotty, I can't do it. It's too direct." The thought of it filled me with anxiety. "I need to test the waters first."

"Okay, give me a minute." Scotty put me on hold.

I heard some sort of discussion going on in the background with Doug, but I couldn't quite discern what was being said because Scotty had covered the mouthpiece with his hand.

"I'll tell you what I'll do," he stated when he came back on the line. "I'll ring him and tell him I have a few pieces that just came in and that I'll send you along with them so he can have a look. This way, if he wants to see you he'll agree, and if not, he'll make up some excuse or other."

"What a brilliant idea!" I felt excited all of a sudden. I now had a genuine excuse to seek him out, but then a thought occurred to me. "Hold on a second. Do you really have something to show him or is this a lot of hogwash?"

"Mainly hogwash, darling," Scotty replied with a smile in his voice. "I have nothing to show him, but Doug has some pieces in his shop that he'll drop off to you this evening so you can see Rick tomorrow. Will this suit?"

"Sure." I sent a silent thanks to Doug. "What pieces are they?"

"A couple of antique tagines and a table lamp. I know Rick'll like them."

"Okay, make the call. Thank you, Scotty, and please thank Doug for me, too." I rang off and whirled around the room with eager anticipation.

I would see Rick again and though I was seeing him on the

pretext of showing him the pieces from the shop, this was my big opportunity to tell him... Tell him what? I stopped the whirling and sat down on the sofa, a frown on my face while I tried to figure out what I would say.

"Oh hi, Rick. I ran into Denise the other day, and she told me you like me. So I now believe you about not being together with her, and I want to marry you... No, I mean, I love you... No, I... Oh, I don't know what I mean!" I played the conversation inside my head until I cried out in frustration, "This won't do! What do I say? How do I bring up the subject?"

I spent the rest of the day trying to come up with a good line with which to open the conversation between us, and by the evening I had a huge headache.

Doug dropped by with the pieces and after taking in my puffy eyes, he ordered me to lie down with a cold compress and made me a cup of chamomile. He stayed with me until I fell asleep.

There was a text message on my mobile the following morning. I must've been in deep slumber when it came through, but as I dragged myself out of bed I saw the notification icon on the phone and opened the message. It was from Scotty and it read: *The eagle has landed. 11.00am at Rick's.* This was accompanied by a smiley icon. I replied, *Thank you* and noticed it was almost ten o'clock.

I rushed to the bathroom and screamed when I saw my face. Though my headache had gone, I had horribly puffy eyes. There was only one thing to do in such a situation. First, I showered, and then rummaged around the bathroom cabinet for hemorrhoid cream. It was the supermodel's trick to de-puff eyes after a night's debauchery. I rarely used the stuff, but since I had read about it in "Secret Beauty Tips", an article in one of Lola's magazines, I always kept a tube at home just in case.

While I gave the cream time to work, I dressed in a flowing white Indian cotton dress, had a strong cup of coffee to wake myself up, and finally went to put on my make-up. I was happy to discover upon closer inspection, that there was very little puffiness left under my eyes, and I sent a big thank you to the supermodels for this wonderful tip.

I was out the door by a quarter to eleven and placed the pieces in my hatchback. Even though Rick's was only a block away from where I lived, I couldn't walk carrying the items as it would've been

159

awkward and I could drop something, hence I had to drive and made it with two minutes to spare.

"Miss Ryan," Mohsen greeted me when I walked in the door, a wide smile of welcome on his dark face, "it's been a long time. Mr Rick told me you were coming around and I was to show you to his office and get the items out of the car."

I smiled back at him. "Thank you, Mohsen. Here are the keys." I gave him my car keys, and he led me to Rick's office, where he knocked on the door and asked me to go in. I hesitated for a moment before turning the door handle and entering the room.

Rick was at his desk, wearing jeans and a white shirt open at the neck. He looked tanned, relaxed, and absolutely drop-dead gorgeous. When he looked up and smiled, my heart started to thump inside my chest. He stood and walked over to me, the scent of his aftershave assaulting my senses and sending the blood coursing through my body.

"Cat, it's great to see you again," he pecked me on the cheek. "I hope you've been well."

I was sure my cheeks were bright red. "I… Yes, thank you. I'm well."

"Would you like something to drink?" His eyes appraised me, and I wanted to dive into his arms and sexually assault him. The thought made me grow very warm.

"Ah, no, no. I'm good." *Stop it, Cat, and get a grip on yourself.*

"In that case, please have a seat." Rick invited, but I remained standing.

"I… um… I…" *Oh, my God, I've lost my mind!* I still had no idea as to what I was going to say to him.

Thankfully, there was a knock on the door and Mohsen walked in with the pieces I brought over. He deposited them carefully on Rick's desk and returned the car keys to me.

"Thank you, Mohsen." Rick nodded at him and proceeded to examine the items. Mohsen gave me a smile and left us alone.

While Rick admired the pieces, I admired him and took in a lung-full of his aftershave. I suddenly felt woozy and stumbled, and if it hadn't been for Rick's quick move, I would have fallen. Instead, I was caught by a pair of arms that brought me close to a hard chest.

I must've looked like a swooning heroine in a romance novel while I clung to him to keep myself from falling. Then, my eyes made contact with his and my mouth parted of its own accord. Rick didn't miss the opportunity, and he kissed me—lightly at first, but then with more force when he felt me reciprocate.

"Oh, Rick," I whispered against his delicious mouth, "I've been such a fool."

He smiled, making my knees wobble. "You have been a fool, Cat Ryan," he declared. "But I love you all the same."

If he hadn't been holding me, I would've definitely fallen to the floor. My heart sang while my legs still felt weak.

"What changed your mind, my love?" he asked gently.

My love! He called me *my love!* I was in seventh heaven. I told him briefly about my encounter with Denise, and this was all he needed to hear. He led me to a chaise lounge at one end of the office and held me in his arms while we reclined into it and kissed hungrily. After a long time, we talked, and I remained within the circle of his arms.

"So no more doubts?" he asked, playing with a strand of my hair. His every touch sent little shivers of delight rushing through my body.

"None at all, but— "

"But what, my love?" He traced the outline of my nose with his fingertip and then moved onto my lips. His eyes gazed into mine, and I could see the love written in them. I forgot what I wanted to say, and I let him kiss me again, this time softly and lingeringly. When his lips lifted from mine, he said, "I'm sure you still have some questions."

Then I remembered. "Well, Rick, in my defense, you must admit the whole thing looked a little suspicious—all those times I saw you with Denise, and then the necklace."

He smiled. "Ah yes, the necklace! Well, let me explain everything to you this time, but I need a coffee first so I can keep my head while we talk. Otherwise, I'm going to make love to you right here and now."

I blushed deeply, and he smiled. He helped us off the chaise lounge and rang for coffee for both of us. While we waited, we kissed some more, and things started to get passionate. We almost returned to the chaise lounge, but there was a knock on the door, and we pulled apart swiftly as a waiter came in with two cappuccinos. Then, we sat side by side on the lounge, and Rick talked while we sipped our drinks.

"The necklace was my gift to Denise for her upcoming state of motherhood," he explained. I was surprised to hear this, but I let him continue. "You see, Denise always wanted children, and I denied her that—first because I was too busy building the business back in New York, and then restarting the business here in Sydney. I was always busy and thought there would be time for kids later, but Denise thought otherwise. Needless to say, our marriage started to deteriorate and we grew apart. We wanted different things, but we remained friends after the divorce. Then, when she met Peter and they had their financial problems, I raised money to help them out." Rick saw the question in my eyes. "You must wonder why I would help them, right?"

I nodded.

"Well, Denise had shares in my business and though we divorced, she never asked for them back. At the time, it would've ruined me if I'd tried to buy her out. The business wasn't established enough. Then, when she and Peter ran into trouble, I was in a position to help them by buying the shares from her. And this is the reason why we met up over a few dinners. Denise thought I was being too generous with what I offered to pay her, but I owed her for being so understanding in the past. Anyway, it took me several meetings to convince her to accept the offer."

While he talked, I fell more and more in love with this rare man. A man who was not only confident and strong, but also one who did right by those he cared about—a man who was fair in his dealings, even with an ex-wife. Indeed, very rare.

The room was silent, and I noticed Rick had stopped talking. He had explained everything, and I had nothing more to say except one thing. I put down my cup, took his from his hand and placed it next to mine, and then put my arms around his neck. "I love you, Rick Blake—even though I can't understand why you're willing to put up with a crazy woman like me." I grinned.

"You mean a woman who dates on the internet and then writes a blog about her experiences?" The look of surprise on my face made him laugh.

"But how—" I started to ask.

"How did I know you were dating under false pretences?" he finished the question for me. I nodded. "Well, I'll tell you if you promise not to get upset."

162

I was too mystified to be upset. "I won't. I promise," I reassured him.

"Scotty made sure I found out," Rick confessed.

I pulled my arms away from around his neck for a moment and gazed straight at him, a look of resolve in my eyes. "When did he do this?"

Rick laughed again. "Oh, no! You're not going to murder him, are you?"

I smirked. "Not if I can help it," I responded with merriment in my voice.

"It was the day I bumped into you and Vincent at Lorenzo's. He admitted you were on a date when I told him I'd seen you with Vincent, who mentioned having met you online. Anyway, I guess Scotty saw the 'little green monster' in my eyes and wanted to ensure I knew it was not a real date," he explained. "He brought up one of your blog posts on his computer so I could read it while he went off to fetch the items I was collecting from him."

"But why didn't he simply tell you straight out about the blog?" I was intrigued.

Rick brought his lips close to mine with a glint of expectation in his eyes. "That's exactly what he did by letting me see it. Besides, it confirmed everything. I mean, you didn't really think I believed all those men you met at the café were clients, did you?"

My look of utter amazement made him laugh once more, and then his arms drew me to him as he said with passion in his voice, "Your craziness is one of your most alluring qualities, my Cat, not to mention your face, your legs, your—"

I smiled suggestively and pressed my lips to his, vowing never to let him go.

Rick pulled me closer and whispered, "Anyway, after the James incident, I knew I had to step in somehow and stop you from inviting more disaster into your life."

"Please, don't even remind me!" I shivered at the thought of James, the lecher; and tightened my hold on Rick. "I have the man I want, and this is all I care about."

Rick's loving smile set my body on fire, and as he brought his lips to mine, he uttered, "My dear, this is the beginning of a beautiful relationship."

The End

About The Author

Sylvia Massara is a multi-genre author based in Sydney, Australia. She loves to dabble in wacky love affairs, drama, murder, sci-fi (or anything else that takes her fancy) over good coffee.

Born in Argentina from Italian and Spanish descent (with a bit of Swiss thrown in) and transplanted to Australia at age 10, Sylvia describes herself as a bit of a "moggie" cat by way of mixed pedigree. She is also a citizen of the world as she has travelled widely throughout most of her life and she's the proud owner of three passports.

From a creative perspective, Sylvia has been writing since her early teens and her work consists of novels, screenplays and freelance writing. She has also dabbled in acting on and off, songwriting and even had her own band during her teens/early 20s where she performed at various venues.

As with most authors, Sylvia draws on her varied experience from the often puzzling tapestry of life. A few years ago Sylvia resigned from the human race because she discovered the animal kingdom was a much nicer place to be.

Currently, Sylvia lives with her cat, Mia; and always vicariously through the many characters in her head. Occasionally, Sylvia ventures into the world of humans, and she cherishes genuine friendships as they are a rare find.

Sylvia has recently released her 7th novel, The Stranger, a sci-fi apocalyptic romance with moralistic issues that involve the fight of love vs evil in the cosmos.

Please visit the author's website to keep up with her latest novels or to contact her at: www.sylviamassara.com

About Massara's Novels

The Mia Ferrari Mystery Series

<u>Playing With The Bad Boys</u>

A woman plunges ten floors down an atrium and lands on a baby grand piano in the luxurious Rourke Hotel Sydney. The police rule this as a straight case of suicide; but 48-year-old hotel duty manager and wannabe investigator, Mia Ferrari, thinks otherwise.

As Mia sets out to unravel the mysterious death and prove the cops wrong, especially her archenemy, Detective Sergeant Phil Smythe; she comes up against an unsavoury cast of characters who will do anything to shut her up. But with a little help from her friends, Mia will not stop until she unearths the truth.

Mia Ferrari is a "wiseass", older chick with determination and an attitude, and she never takes "no" for an answer.

<u>The Gay Mardi Gras Murders</u>

Mia Ferrari, smartarse, older chick, super sleuth, is back in her 2nd murder mystery, and this time, she is up to her neck in drag queens, a rare diamond with a curse and murder most foul against the backdrop of Sydney's world famous Gay Mardi Gras.

A female impersonator is found dismembered in her hotel suite bathtub, and a rare diamond worth twenty million dollars is gone. The Gay Mardi Gras is fast approaching and Mia Ferrari, senior duty manager of the exclusive Rourke International Hotel Sydney, has to juggle a bunch of drag queens, a number of fabulously handsome gay men, a transsexual with a dark mystery, a young cop with sex on his mind, a close friend from the UK who is having marital problems and a mounting body count.

As Mia pits her investigative skills against her archenemy, Detective Sergeant Phil Smythe, to solve the case, she not only becomes embroiled in the life of the people around her, but it looks like she is the next target for a serial killer with a grudge against gay men.

The South Pacific Murders

It's a well-known fact that wherever Mia Ferrari goes trouble always follows, and going on a holiday cruise to Hawaii is no different.

A killer is on the loose onboard ship. A number of doctors from a medical convention are being murdered one by one. The captain of the cruise liner asks Mia and her travelling companions to take over the investigation while the ship is in the middle of the Pacific Ocean toward its final destination. A secret sex club and horse racing bets are the only clues that can uncover the identity of the killer, but will Mia be able to solve the mystery before the killer strikes again?

Join Mia and her friends, plus her sexy detective archenemy, on a cruise to murder, mayhem, and sizzling hot sex.

Science fiction romance

The Stranger

The Stranger is a sci-fi apocalyptic romance with moralistic issues involving the fight between love and evil and its repercussions.

Rhys is on a mission on Earth in order to determine Earth's destiny, but his judgement is in danger of becoming clouded when he meets and falls in love with Carla, a human. The balance of life on Earth depends upon Rhys's recommendation to the League of Galaxies. But how will Rhys choose between his mission and his love for an Earthling? Rhys is forced to weigh up the collective evil on Earth and its causal effect on the greater good of other life in the universe against the love he has for one woman.

This is not simply a tale of love between two beings but a story of the unconditional and sublime love, which is the force that drives the cosmos.

The Stranger was dedicated to the Loving Memory of David Bowie.

Romance

Like Casablanca

What does internet dating and Casablanca have in common? Nothing, unless you go to Rick's Cafe and find out what antiques dealer and dating blogger, Cat Ryan, is up to.

Cat's doing research for her internet dating blog gig, and the place she chooses to meet her many dates is at Rick's Cafe in Sydney. But what of its disturbingly handsome owner, Rick Blake?

Cat wonders what he thinks, seeing her with a different male all the time. What's more, why does this bother Cat so much? It's not like she wants any involvement after her recent break up with Josh, her cheating ex. Besides, it looks like Rick is trying to get back together with his ex-wife, Denise. So Cat decides to play it safe, but her heart has different ideas.

The Other Boyfriend

Sarah Jamison is on a mission to find a boyfriend for Moira, who is her lover's partner. And Sarah's best friend, Monica, comes to the rescue with the perfect solution. Enter the enigmatic Mike Connor. Monica is sure that Mike will sweep Moira off her feet, leaving the way open for Sarah to be with her true love, Jeffrey.

Sarah hates Mike on sight despite the fact that her body tells her otherwise. He is a romance novel "hero-type" who is smug and full of himself. But the only way to accomplish her mission is for her to work with Mike so she can be together with the man she loves.

Jeffrey has promised her that the minute he can end his platonic relationship with Moira, he will be with Sarah for good; but he is having trouble letting go of the wretched woman, and Sarah feels her time is running out. She is terrified of the pending big "M" (menopause), and seeing as she's just turned forty, and her hormones are driving her to do insane and desperate things, she is sure that it is not too far off into the future!

So here she is, building a multi-level marketing business in Taiwan, and struggling with it all: a stranger in a foreign country, away from her mother and friends back in London; a reluctant lover; a drop-dead gorgeous man who might have ulterior motives for helping her, and finally, a business that seems to be dwindling.

Sarah is doing it all in the name of love and the last chance to have a family, and if this means scheming and working with the devil himself, then she will do it! What she doesn't take into account is the fact that instead of getting closer to her goal, Sarah's feelings take a turn, and she finds herself increasingly thinking about the very man she despises the most – "the other boyfriend".

Contemporary fiction – drama

The Soul Bearers

Partly inspired by true life events, this is a story of courage, the gift of friendship, and unconditional love. The story involves three people whose lives cross for a short period of time and the profound effect that results from their interaction.

Alex, a freelance travel writer and victim of child abuse, arrives in Sydney in an attempt to exorcise the ghosts of her past. She shares a house with Steve and the disturbing Matthew, a homosexual couple. Alex finds herself inexplicably attracted to Matthew and she must battle with her repressed sexuality and fear of intimacy. Matthew, an aspiring actor, must face the prospect of a potential future without his partner, who has AIDS, and he must deal with the rejection of his socialite parents.

Steve is the rock to which the troubled Matthew and Alex cling while they examine their lives and beliefs in the hope that they will find the strength to face their pain and release the past.

This powerful story explores the true meaning of unconditional love and friendship.